YOU ARE MY SERENDIPITY

Priyanka Varma

First published in 2020 by

Becomeshakespeare.com

One Point Six Technologies Pvt. Ltd.
119-123, 1st floor, Building No. J2, Wadala East,
Wadala Truck Terminal, Mumbai, Maharashtra 400037, India
T: +91 8080226699

ISBN - 978-93-90040-73-5

ABOUT THE AUTHOR

PRIYANKA VARMA is a graduate of University Of Western Ontario, Toronto, Canada. She has lived in India, Middle East and Canada in her lifetime. She has done her schooling from Sacred Heart - Jamshedpur, Indian School Muscat - Oman and Milliken Mills High School - Canada.

In addition to her ferver for writing, she is a trained finance professional. She has worked for leading organizations such as Astral Media and Union Bank Of Switzerland in Toronto as an analyst.

Her first novel, The Rite To Love, was pubished in November of 2015. It was based on her observations on a live-in relationship with a backdrop of morsels of being married. Contrasting the two with the barometer of being accepted. She has also blogged for TOI (Times of India), published her book of poems, Genesis, in 2015, and other books such as Women of the Millenium and Confessions Of A Workoholic, pubished in 2018 and 2019 respectively.

Currently, and infinitely ever, relishing in the realm of motherhood. She is a mom to her 8 year-old, daughter named Aanya.

In the future, she would like to publish more books. Professionaly, she is working as an HR specialist with an MNC.

You walked in with your convictions,
with dreams in your eyes,
My life was nothing but a delft blue, cloudless night
that you piroutted into a star-lit sky...

To you, my love, I dedicate this book...

- Priya

SYNOPSIS

You're always one decision away from a different life. According to me, progress is impossible without a change and that cannot change and those that cannot change their minds cannot change anything. Great learning experiences never come from comfort. Learning experiences can come in many forms in our lives. It might come strongly like a tidal wave, or creep in gradually like a molten volcano. It can make you foresee grave tragedies, decide between difficult choices, be vary of broken relationships or be excited about new opportunities. But its all in your mindset.

As you approach such a decision, that can change your mindset, that voice inside you might say, /"are you sure you can do it?" Your mindset helps you interpret those decisions. If you have a growth mindset, then you will approach the tough decisions with ramped up strategies and effort, expand yourself and your abilities.

A good strategy is to build on two factors – time and effort as you fuel your journey and then you hone your talent, skills, abilities to garner a positive outcome of your decision. Take feedback constructively and always know that it isn't really about the decision but about the journey of life.

Tanya's 9-year journey across several continents was a success because of her positive mindset, piroutted through a life-changing strategy. She kept following it with confidence, faith and positivity. Her decisions after moving across continents wasn't so much about proving a point but it was about proving to herself about her abilities. Whether she became triumphant is for the readers to decide. She is content, her journey continues....

CHAPTER 1

She hurriedly put her "standard signature" below her long email, which was actually supposed to be her resignation letter. It had been a year in this gruel some role as an analyst. She managed to topple over this position, after meeting up with an "impressionable" man. Was he impressionable? Wouldn't seem so considering where she met him.

It was on a morose winter night at an upscale hookah bar with a quartet singing 90s pop acapellas in the background with Hindi lyrics. So, by the atmosphere, it was pretty evident that the crowd was a mix of East and West. The composition could be broken down between three ethnic groups - European, Moroccan and Indo-western. Very much chattering in the mint-Canadian accent and discussing Canadian Politics (the Caucasian way) but very much in an identity crisis because of their unpronounceable names and overtly traditional, first-generational parents that wouldn't think twice about batting their eyelids around all corners of the vertex until the retinas popped out in dismay at their lifestyles.

That's where Tanya was, hanging out with her girls. Jiving to the entrancing tunes that made her putty in the hands of an elongated trunk like structure that breathed scents and earthiness of the Himalayan mountains. Entranced in the atmosphere, there lay a confusion between a dreary career and a so-so love life, which made her just want to intoxicate and fall asleep. The career and the love-life actually had similar characteristics, it could both be progressive if they were given attention, detail and focus. They would require for you to be patient but also have a strategy in mind. Lastly, be bold enough to know when its time to switch to a better option. It was that time in Tanya's life, where she was at this crucial juncture. When was she ever gonna have the dream man and a dream job??

Then came this guy in an Armani, checkered shirt and black pants, almost shadowing the dim red lamp that had lit up the room. He leaned over and introduced himself to everyone at the table. The girls quite liked his first move, first round of drinks is a surefire "you can join us and charm us."

We drank and sipped as we laughed at his slightly tweaked Russell Peters jokes. Very repetitive yet very dry. Then his gaze got fixed onto this dazy-eyed Tanya as she was rather distracted. They got to talking about her work and hobbies. He was working for this superlatively, famous bank with good perks and not to mention a big booster on his CV. He offered Tanya an opportunity to work at the bank as he could sense she became more disinterested and gulped her drink at once when asked to describe her job.

His promises seemed like those sprouty fortune cookies that would make you chuckle for like two minutes and then seem to become a whiff in the air. She took down his email address and made it a point to spruce up her CV and send it over to this chap named Ankit Dube she met last night. She sent it even before she made her morning coffee and that was totally epic. "Billing Analyst" was the job title and it seemed like a much-esteemed promotion from the "accountant/analyst" role that she had worked in for two years. He wondered why he had offered to help. It could be because he wanted another "Indian" person in the office so that they could reprise all those Russell Peters jokes, relish in those kathi rolls and kebabs from the corner store that timely dispelled off savoury scents from 2pm onwards.

A week later, a quick three rounds of interviews and she was hired. She then bumped into Ankit in the hallways and they went out for drinks to celebrate. The job seemed quite gruelsome but the guy was moderately entertaining. A respite from the fast-paced and somewhat chastening world of money-making (pun intended). If New York or Chicago offices called in for an updated report, then you would have to immediately switch from your main excel spreadsheet with umpteen linked numbers into your subsidiary ones and create a mini report from the data gathered within all the linked sheets, double-check, write a four-sentence analysis and send it immediately. Besides this, there were monthly billing schedules, printing invoices and constantly communicating with our clients that held her up until about 7pm each night. Then it was out and about for dinner and drinks with her gals Truly, she was leading the downtown life, highlighted with three D's – Divas, Deadlines and Daiquiris.

But, after a while she found herself to be in the same roundabout of life -> work and life becoming really repetitive, not progressing anywhere. The guys her age weren't feeling the body-clock and didn't want to go beyond second-base. She wanted a change in life. She was yearning for responsibilities, priorities that gave her self-worth. She wanted to look after a man, be his muse, his anchor, his laughter-therapy and momma to babies that looked just like him.

At 27, was she ever gonna find this Adonis that she had dreamed of. She didn't realize but her life was waiting in the wings, about to take flight of a lifetime.

CHAPTER 2

Her boss wasn't ready to accept the fact that she was going to resign. She was doing some great work on the analysis front, also her work on the billing-side had been on-schedule where as her predecessors had always garnered some delay or another. She entered his office for a final good bye, she chose to wear this bright-yellow, flowery, peasant top and beige flared pants. Her hair was straightened, her Nine-West, suede boots were a great accessory and her pearls were really the cherry on the cake. It was a perfectly-coordinated outfit for the last day at work.

"Hello Tanya, common in. You're feeling OK? The last two weeks have been really a shocker for all of us. You've dropped a whopper on us to say the least."

"Yes I needed this change and I'm very happy, Mr. Hahmann." Sven Hahmann, she was pretty sure, had hired her at first sight. He had a liking for "exotic women". By exotic we mean it was any skin-tone on the left of the "beige" on MAC cosmetics compact list (2008). That and black, long hair. It wasn't a lie, his team of women could actually be defined as a group of contestants for Miss Universe 2008. But with great analytical skills and willing to please him with spicy, home-made meals.

Tanya also managed to have a great connection with him. She learnt alot of the "tricks of the trade" and the way to speak and handle anxious clients. The wealthier the clients, the more risk they were willing to take. Thus the more compassionate and "air hostessy" nice you needed to be. His words of wisdom were definitely something she was gonna miss. But, at this moment, she was completely enamoured with this guy she was about to get married to.

She had forgotten everything else in the world. Her surroundings, Toronto, seemed like a foreign land. A city that was pulling her away from the man she had dreamed of. He was it.

At 27, she was glad she had waited to speak to him. Not to say the "frogs" weren't worth the time and the mini-dresses and the long hours on the phone, but they sure made her realize that a good guy was worth the wait. Great conversations were the reason she was attracted to him. At 29, he was self-assured, career-oriented, and he valued her opinions. He wasn't self-assured because he was rich, but because he had his head in the right place. He wasn't yearning for constant attention from any women willing to provide the kind of support he needed to fulfill his a,bitions. He wanted her to just be the spectator while he ran the show. She was so enamoured that she didn't mind while, with guys in her previous relationships, they wanted her to be available at the drop of the hat. Whether it was a family-dinner night or a friend's bridal shower, or a deadline at work. She often had to disappoint alot of important people at work and her parents just so he could meet these guys. This "pull" was rather condescending and annoying. This also meant that she would have to forgo alot in the future for them. So then that meant no pretesting for a ring in the future. She wasn't gonna have it. She liked the fact that she was really individualistic in that way. This guy, that had just proposed to her, had opened up an entirely new perspective to her. That it wasn't the place, but the person that mattered. She was told by alot of people that long-distance relationships don't work in the long-run and aren't practical. It was more like "out of sight" and "out of mind". But for her, it was good that way. The attraction was such that she looked ahead to speaking to him every night.

She eagerly picked up the anxiousness in his voice about these exams he was gonna write. All his college-mates were writing it with him, so they would collectively study together. So when he got time to speak to her, he would just shed his fears on her.

The beginning of a relationship is when the bearings are tested the most. There might be alot of differences, getting accustomed to each others temperaments, likes, dislikes and routines altogether. It's because the barometer of each relationship works on the pressures caused by being attracted to one another. You are so bent on being with one another that the more attracted you are to the other person, the more you will make it work.

For Tanya, it was being attracted to him that defied all concerns and notions about deciding to marry a person that was half-way across the world. The most exalting thing about it was that he hadn't curbed her in any way. She felt just as liberated, worked long hours, worked out, hung out with friends and felt that this relationship was trying to elicit the best out of her.

She was, herself, a bohemian at heart, had the spirit of a butterfly, and wanted to discover the world and then just end up at home only at night. At her age, she wasn't trying to be superwomen, but only testing the nascent waves of adulthood and independence.

Plus, each time he called, she felt special. She felt like she could positively contribute to his life without having to forgo her priorities.

She did have a few insecurities with regards to her career, and the fact that she was too submissive towards men (her Bohemianism and the fact that she was easygoing also). He gave her the confidence that she could just leave everything, also, be removed from her comfort zone and be able to manage her married life. Be that support system he was looking for. That was a big position to manage, and she felt that she deserved that coveted crown. The more protected she felt in her father's home and her friend circles, the more liberated she felt in his voice. The more he appreciated the fact that she was bohemian in her ways. The one thing that he hadn't picked up on was that she was very "ditsy". She was particular, she loved wondering around high-end designer stores and had a zest for weird, exotic dishes. Every girl had a mysterious side to her and this was hers. She revelled in her own company. She loved being alone. Loneliness gave her the chance to be strong, be in tune with herself and to gather her thoughts. He gave direction to her wavering mind. At 27, she had realized that they were poles apart and very much yearning to be a couple. He didn't want her to curb her ways, but she was willing to become totally Indian for him.

Was her father willing to let her go? Unlike her past relationships, he was the one that initiated it, and he was surprised that she wanted to marry him.

Question is, what was his name? His name was Rohan Mathur. The man that would hold the switch to the next nine years of life. Had Rohan Mathur realized what had hit him?? Tanya wasn't gonna disclose it just yet.

CHAPTER 3

S o, it had been about a month since she had made it official about her impending wedding. Her parents were experiencing the "birth pangs" once again with the wedding preparations, making frantic calls to their relatives in Delhi, Patna and Jamshedpur. They were jubilant also, but just like the birth-pangs, they would finally breathe a sign of contentment once they entire process had ended.

For a father, what did it mean to wed your daughter? Tanya could sense a tone of chirpiness in his voice and also contrarily his eyes would moisten each time she would iron his shirt for work, make him dinner, or help him shovel the snow in the backyard. She was his "man friday" for all tasks.

Right from the time she was about four years old, she could accompany him to his office on Sundays. Why Sundays? Because the office was quite, the staff wasn't there and he could make her part of his work. Just so he could relish his two loves at once – work and his firstborn. She would fetch him a glass of water from the filter, arrange all the pens in his drawers, make him an "i love you" card and sit on his lap and wonder at the procreation of a PC.

What did he want to accomplish with her? He wanted to depict to her that she was willing to be around. He had barmy hours at work and he often had to travel to Lucknow and Kolkatta. During Eid, he would bring bright shiny clothes and kebabs specially for her. Also, for her, during Christmas, he would shower her with pastries and cakes. As much as his work was filled with travel, deadlines and touring, he wanted to make sure he was OK with it. All those times that he was "missing" in the scenes, he wanted to make-up for them. Wherever he went, he bought gifts and trinkets for her. He wanted to show her that she was an important part of his life. By this, he set an example of a man that truly loved her, very early on in her life. A man, if he wants you in his life, makes an effort to make you feel special. You become a vital tile in the mosaic of his life. Thus, Tanya learnt to be valued and made special in a man's company. She learnt that her presence in his life was just as meaningful as his in her life. An even sum. A dime for a dime, when you're relationships are equal, then you're opinions are valued and you feel appreciated. The ting and the yang come together to make a happy and fulfilling relationship. Once this guideline is followed, then you don't settle for less. That's why it had taken Tanya a good 27 years to decide to marry Rohan.

When getting to know Rohan, she followed the blueprint ingrained in her memory, of her father's behaviour towards her. She didn't have to yearn for his attention, he called her duly at a certain time and they spoke. Though they spoke about the usual things – sports, news, law, analytics, her liking for him became stronger. He was never vulgar with her, never tried to seduce her with dirt (usually located in disputable, another legal term, kind of films). She didn't initiate it either. She wanted him to see her in person first. He didn't have any preconceived notions about her past, he was only interested in her future, in her well-being and the way he suited her life. She was enamored, but he had to be attracted to her body in order to get physical with her. That was her opinion.

Connections with that special someone isn't just psychology or biology. It does start with the brain though. Being just about 3 pounds, its regarded as the most exciting organ in the human body, that's gotta make it quite a competent and simulating one when compared to other 3--pounders in the body!! Our brain begins to work overtime because we need to become that person that is consistently accepting, caring and compassionate with ourselves. We need to become strong from within, to be able to handle another's bad day. We need to locate that strength from within to stay openhearted in the face of fear and conflict from our loved ones. The stronger we are, the more reliable we will be to cushion off the turbulence in our relationships.

CHAPTER 4

((Tanya, take my card, take out 150 dollars, and get it for me please. We have to go to Gerrard Street to begin the Canada part of the wedding shopping,' she hollered out as Tanya made her way out to the garage with a bagel in one hand and an empty coffee mug in another. Gerrard Street, the focal point of all of the nostalgia and

The coffee mug was to be filled at the end of her subway ride at union station. On her subway rides, she would usually listen to her favourite tunes to get into the zone of working 9-hour days. The top three on her list were usually Jay-Z's fiesta or R. Kelly's ignition or Mariah Carey's Fantasy".Her journey on these subway rides had begun three years ago when she got her first job out of university. Her train rides were like bitter-sweet moments, like those sour-gold bears from Haribos. The bitter parts were the repetitive feeling of being all charged up in the mornings, trying to get focused, and then being very consumed and worn-out in the evenings on the way back home. The sweet part was the fellow-passengers, her interactions with them and watching life unfold at different stages – a young lad commuting to university all burried in his textbooks to a young mother rocking a stroller back-and-forth so that her infant would sleep through the long ride and then watching an old couple rush in hand-in-hand with a cinnabon in their hands so that they could share it on a cold winter night. The bitter parts taught her consistency and the sweet parts taught her to handle the fluidity and impermanence in life.

These days, it was all about her journey ahead. Going from East to West was a different ballgame altogether. She had heard and seen of brides move from the East to West, that is from India to United States or Canada, but hers was the reverse. They had to make very poignant changes so that they could adjust to the new environment, different people, adopt different values and become an intricate part of society. It was actually, the same way around. But, whether you went from a sari-clad, high-end designer in South Delhi to New York or from the suburbs of Canada to Pune or Bangalore, if you were Indian, you had to be the quintessential "Bahu". You had to just not be the woman of your man's dreams, but the man of everyone's dreams. This was the time to don your various different personalities and charm everyone. It wasn't like Tanya was put-off by the traditions and the expectations, but she realized that if she married a Greek man or a Guyanese fella, it would be more of a "disputable" (pun intended) situation because the culture would be different altogether. The roots of each country were as seeped in you as the genes in your DNA. The familiarity when you enter an Indian home, be it in India, Botswana, London, Dubai or Chicago, chances are you would be greeted with a Lord Ganesha statue at the entrance, served Neembu Paani or Aam Panna on a hot summer evening, you would gorge on delicacies made with Desi Ghee and ground, pungent spices and lastly discuss Indian politics and "First Night" experiences in the same breath, tone and manner. So, this familiarity was great when you had to make a life-changing decision such as marriage.

The familiarity was also great conversation-starter between Tanya and Rohan, and Rohan was a big-time foodie. This familiarity also helped them carve out a portrait for the future. The hues and the figurines in the portrait embodied their desires, wants and wishes.

They were bonded for life. In good times and in times that had the potential to change into good forever.

Soon she reached her destination as the train reached union station. She rushed out along with the crowds that raced in towards work, Tanya first raced for coffee. She knew that Delhi had Starbucks, Costa Coffee and various brands, but Tim Hortons would be missing. But hey, the high she got from speaking to her Adonis was the best thing ever. It was like a double-chocolate latte and then some!

There was so much in common between coffee and men! Coffee was dependable, so was Rohan. Even before we're old enough to drive, we were grabbing vanilla-caramel, creamy concoctions with friends and feeling like life had reached its peak. Speaking to Rohan every night made her realize that she had reached a peak of enlightenment. It wasn't an enlightenment that made her feel equal. Just the way you feel with friends. It was a feeling of unity that occureed when she saw herself in Rohan. He brought a lot of value to her life. There is no time of the day a coffee can't improve, and sometimes its hard to describe the feeling we get for the beloved drink that picks us up in a way that nothing else can. The same was the case with Rohan. Be it an argument with her boss on a current revenue analysis, or a bickering with her brother, about which Raptors tickets to book for playoffs, a phone-call from Rohan and her day would just brighten up. He made sense of the situations and gave her solutions so she wouldn't have to think for himself. He was just making it more simple to fall in love with him.

CHAPTER 5

It was that time of the month! No! No! Not when aunt flow was to visit, but the time of the monthly kitty party of women of 'Bihar Association Of Canada'. Just like aunt flow, these were unavoidable but also a time when you can relish on all the delicacies you wanted. These kitties entailed an elaborate food menu (the cuisine was of the choice of the host), usually based on the theme. Oh! There had to be a theme. This time it was at Alka's house (Alka was Tanya's mother) and the theme was "Wedding Fever.' Given the occasion of the impending wedding. Alka had decorated their family room, with a lot of silk fabrics. The panels for the curtains on the windows were draped around in waves of Kanjeevaram silk sarees. She had purchased some silk cushions also, and a rug made from red ikkat fabric with gota-work on it. It was a dinner so the garage and the entrance were decorated with string lights! The ones the neighbourhood only got to see during Christmas time! So, instantly, the ladies began to feel festive and excited.

For welcome drinks, Alka had made Fresca Sangrias, it truly got the ladies to be on a high! The ladies were also greeted with a dholki and ghungroos to sing wedding songs. So the songs ranged from "Main Sasural Nahi Jaaongi" from Chandni to folk songs like, "Banna Mera Phool Ghulab". There was also a mehendi-waali for the occasion. The Indian Beauticians in Canada didn't actually run their own parlors or work in parlors (cuz they have a problem listening to a "Phoren" woman boss's instructions). They work as an independent professional. Their parlors are usually in the basements of their homes. So they don't really have to pay "taxes" cuz they haven't registered their business and they are also earning money on the sly. One of the many traits that Indians are famous for no matter where they are in the world. So, for our neighborhood, it was Lynn! The name was of-course a Western name but she was Assamese. She had immigrated with her husband and children 15 years back just like many of us. Her sprightly smile that made her eyes sink into her cheeks gave her cherub face a more pleasant and affable feel. She was superbly sharp in her skills, so we loved her even more. She had dressed according to the occassion in an olive-green sharara and golden dupatta. She also sang along as she was stationed in a comfy corner of the family room, charming us with her innovative designs.

Tanya adorned a beaded, rose-pink saree with her mum's exquisite pearl set. She sat, beaming, amongst the ladies that were more inquisitive about her conversations with Rohan than a baby is when given a sweet mango to eat for the first time. They completely devoured her conversations with Rohan and began to relish in the ambrosial nectar of the "minute" details of the romance. Tanya also got alot of feedback on the way to handling Indian men. To get to know or to truly understand the men from the country, you have to know what the country actually stands for. There were three points that popped up like bubbles while garnering all this wisdom from the women. Firstly, Indian men are the most educated of the lot. So, guaranteed they would be in really high paying jobs. For that, they would have to work really hard, which meant, you have to be a great support system and keep them well-fed. Secondly, they love engaging conversations, cuz about 70% of them are well-read, thus their IQ levels could match up-to the elite of the world. To win them over, you would also have to be well-read, knowledgeable, up with the news specially regarding the country's lawmakers, cricket and trade. Nothing makes for an intelligent woman that can support her intuitions and make them into reality.

Lastly, speaking of seduction, India was also the land of the Kamasutra, so the men are ready to put theory to test. Typically, Indian women are taught to be coy, shy and subtle when making sexual advances at men. That is an irony on its own.

Ladies of the 20th century, we have realized that the Kamasutra wasn't a concept to please men so that you feel lesser than them. It gives you the power to please your man in the most generous way possible. The point to note is that it isn't a tool to lure men but it makes you feel desired and wanted also. Its great when you get praised for your brains through your good marks in school and appraisals at work. Or when you get praised for excelling at your hobbies such as knitting, cooking and sports. But its a different thrill altogether when the man makes love to you because he wants you. He loves you and he appreciates you. Its because from the moment women are born, they are criticized about their bodies. Be it a scar in the form of a birthmark, a mole right in the middle of the nose, your complexion or your knobby knees, you are taught to be perfect all your flaws. You have to overcome all your prejudice (that can cause alot of anxieties) in order to feel confident. So Kamasutra gives you the confidence to make you feel like those Kohinoor diamonds. Your body is the result of Science (your DNA) but you get to "own it" with this art of seduction. So, as chivalrous, protective and supportive Indian men are, you really get to become the queen in their eyes when you become intimate with them.

CHAPTER 6

Patio season was in full swing and the divas (in their chatoyant summerwear) were ready to make the most of it. Tanya was having the finest summer of her life with 10 months of solid work experience, one that she could surely build on, and she was engaged to be married. This was a good juncture to be at almost 28 years old. But, also at this age, she had the semi-wisdom to know that she hadn't achieved it alone, she had her own 'a tribe called quest' which she leaned on and they were her true critics. The infamous tribe consisted of four vigorous and ambiguous women that provided much assortment with their refreshing opinions and even when they were quiet, their aura was just as good as the positive vibes you get around a historic monument like the Colosseum. Even when there are no people around and its about to break dawn, the sounds that resonate from the sporadic gush of winds or the sulking of the walls gorged with such rich history give you such confidence that life isn't about giving up but about being strong and timeless like the monument.

Your own city is like your child. It can't ever be too perfect because its identity is embedded in your existence like your identity is in your child's features, mannerisms and thoughts. It has its flaws, but, you tend to overlook them because it provides a balming like quality amongst the uncertainity of the future. You become so protective about it that you subconsciously begin to dissolve yourself into its continuity and repetitions. Days, years, decades can go by and your confidence also continues to resonate from the secluded as well as the lively corners of the city that you belong to. Sometimes, someone, from a foreign city, albeit the same kind of upbringing as you needs to jolt you in a way that gives you a different perspective. Their first meeting was of the similar kind. He was from England, so he could relate to the city's fondness for its history, but, his opinions on what was beneficial and what was a deterrant towards its growth, leading owards Tanya's growth, made her think otherwise. He wasn't criticizing, he couldn't be mean, because he was a doctor. He just made the city's concerns real and ingestible, certainly not in a condescending way. That was what she could recollect from their first meeting...

Toronto, was her like parent. It never gave her false hopes, but rather gave her stern lessons in life, so she became much stronger and also much rooted in its guidance. The seasons were definitely continual, but, her growth was gradual yet different because circumstances were different. She became more and more accustomed to its trials and tribulations and glorified its benefits. Today the benefit was a bright, crispy summer afternoon.

It was also about celebrating Toronto's shortest season with a resounding confidence and heightening our senses with new delicacies. To truly bask in the two months of it's warmth that made you reminisce with familiarity and the city just celebrating this time with spilling out in various festivals and events that made you feel like you were in a new place every year. A much needed respite

Tanya was waiting at this glossy and sun-kissed patio of a restaurant called Gusto. The decor simulated a rustic car mechanic's garage-turned Italian favourite with a usual and street style patio. The casualness of it made you relaxe instantly and retractable glass-ceiling gave it an uncommon and distracting factor. She was waiting for her friends for a delectable lunch time.

First, Heena walked in with two of her most of her prominent accessories- her signature Louis Vuitton Bag and her pearly whites that poured out into the most syrupy smiles ever. She was truly what we call a cross-cultural child with a very progressive family. She had the best of tradition, religion and modernity. Her parents were the "creme de la creme" in Pakistan. She had politics and feudadalism running through her veins, just like her doe-shaped eyes and Angelina Jolie lips. Pakistani women are quite hot-blodded, and very much not submissive as people might perceive. She was depicting exactly that, but in a very metrosexual way (yes that's a term that's used commonly for men only, but aren't we preaching equality everywhere anyway?) In Toronto, though, instead of brashly debating or protesting, she chose to voice her opinions towards racism and women's issues through education. Her primed degree in law and human rights were her sharpest weapons towards a better world for women. Though she was a bit intimidating for the guys, but her bosses loved her. She came in to give me a big hug, and I instantly got a pleasant whiff of her zesty perfume, 'Anais Anais'. "What's with you? You just can't stop smiling? I'm gonna have to cross-examine this one. Since he's all the way in brainy-land." She almost squealed, unlike other gurls, she never screamed. "My little tid-bits have been the talk of tbe town since 24 got a five-star rating from all corners of the world. I'm just really trying to gain clarity in my thoughts and trying to get some sleep as I'm super excited. Zara walked in just minutes later, walking on her toes in order to manage her balance on the groovy surface, just like she was managing a budding career in law. Three years in law school bad made her much less weary of the future, much less un-coordinated with style and much less uneducated. She was the perfect example of a caterpiller transforming into a butterfly in the most graceful way ever, with humility and hardwork. Overcoming traditional beliefs was just like a breeze compared to overcoming her inner fears and her search for her own identity. Being the eldest of four vibrant children, she often had to put her needs aside in order to raise the rest of them. So, when she came out of law school, all primed and shiny, we were truly very proud of her. Takers (suitors) were plenty, but she was too excited about the strides she was making as an attorney. So while she was forging her independence, she was really perplexed about why Tanya would leave her independent life and move half-way across the world to marry a stranger. She leaned over to give Tanya a kiss and told her, "You got the glow! And it isn't even a ring or an undisclosed pregnancy!" In a hurry to reply quickly, she said, ''He gives me the freedom to be the person I want to be. I'm gonna be at lunch with you guys for another hour-and-half and there won't be even one phone-call from him about my whereabouts. That's the security I am liking." She also added, "but when we do talk, he knows I hear him out and listen to him. That's the confidence and trust he has in me."

The three of them got onto ordering the signature drinks for the week, called SPF daiquiris, truly making their bodies rise to nth temperatures with just the name. Tanya made one quick phone-call to Tessa and Shikha to locate their whereabouts. Tess was just parking and Shikha was just getting off the subway. Shania Twain's "You're still the one" was the song of the minute, gently seeping into her ears just like white-sand seeps into your toes awakening all your senses as you unwind on a holiday. She felt so reprised at the moment, yet the song had the familiarity of soul-food. Speaking of soul-food, she just dived for the southern fried, creamy nachos. Just as she looked from that big-bite, she saw Tessa rushing in next, looking just as crisp in her skinny jeans and crop-top. Tessa was the best visually-pleasing example of genes and consonance. Her half-Portugese, half-Indian heritage hadn't just made her a prized possession, but it was more her subdued manners and being practical that rounded-off her whole "desirability" factor towards men. Every time they stepped out, it was like an onslaught of men eyeing her just as an onslaught of bees flocking around honey. She was their bait when they didn't want to be held-up in long lines at clubs, wanted free passes at Carribean events (cuz she was their top-dancer) and also a ride back home from random guys at wee hours from questionable parties and undisclosed events. Above all this, she was a true girl's girl. She was always the first to wish you on your birthday, have a part-time job ready for you at her mother's store and you could always sleep over at her house when some ruckus took place with your parents in your house. She just helped without questioning, she didn't care for reasoning with you. Her quiet yet assuring presence gave you so much confidence cuz there wasn't any criticism in any form of questioning. Instead there was this positive push towards brushing off your mistakes and focusing on growth towards a stronger person. Criticisms can often lead to self-doubt and misleading perceptions. They are like the odd red pimple that pops on your wedding day (right in the middle of your nose) that can't be concealed with either enhanced make-up or extensive lighting. A complete bummer and a bigger knock-down towards your self-esteem. She plops herself right next to Tanya and whips out her phone to show her pictures of these pencil skirts that were made from these silk sarees and had mirror-work on them. "Don't these look great? Fusion is the way to go these days." Tanya got distracted and Tanya got excited, "They are fitted and the flow gives you that traditional feel too. I can pair it up with a collared shirt or a crop-top like yours." Tanya had okayed it.

Shikha hugged her from the back and gave her shoulder a gentle nudge from her right shoulder, " to bring you back to reality, my dear." Tanya gave it a chuckle as she knew that her feet were firmly planted on the ground and she had real expectations from herself. Shikha, everyone knew, had come for the pumpkin-pie Sangrias, but was willing to try out the SPF's. She tried to portray that she was at places and events with them only for the "thrills and frills" but only they knew that she actually cared for them. That beneath her tough exterior, she cared for us like an overprotective father and loving mother, Unlike Tess, that never actually delved into their concerns, she initiated conversations about the "iffy" areas in their lives. It was a trait that she inherited from her tough, entrepreneurial father that had it very tough in his life. He had to uproot his family from the high societies of Delhi so that they could lead a normal life in Toronto, sheltered from the glitz and glam of his Bollywood connections. She was a "Topper" (the Indians will get it) in school, in university and the girls knew she would soon own her own accountancy firm by the time she hit 30. Her drive towards perfection and the fact that she had the ability to pick you apart and then catch you right away made her like a magician that gave you perspective.

Before she knew it, they were busy taking pictures of themselves cuz social media had to be updated on their whereabouts, they had to let everyone know of all the bling they were wearing, of all this new food they had ordered and that being under the radar for brown girls was "so-90s". Speaking of basking in the glory of a new season, these four girls were the perfect example of the four seasons that we get to experience. Summer, spring, autumn and winter can be very different in characteristics but work together in harmony to so that you can cross-boundaries and feel one. They also provoke many changes around the world – such as vegetation, temperatures and people immigrating for a better life. Change is what is the undercurrent of such events. Change for the better, change in conquest of an enriched life, change to cause change in others so that they can augment your life and make the world a more sustainable and inhabitable place to live in for future generations.

CHAPTER 7

Tanya was kind of 70-30 on plane rides. Ever since she first got on a plane when she was all of four years old (as part of a wedding party), sitting right beside the bride's mother who was hysterical and almost about to faint. Her face was roofed in tears and just when the plane ricochet from a dense cloud, aunty Geeta's mouth tossed out the 'bidaai' goodies in form of slippery, baby-vomit mixed with uncompressed snort right onto Tanya's lap. Tanya had to endure the entire hour-long flight with wet clothes and a stench that numbed her sinuses. Since then, she had lived in three countries, travelled quite a bit and had planned to settle down in Paris so she could travel even more, if only Rohan hadn't come across her life. So even if the beginning of her "love saga" with the world had begun with a sour inceptive, it hadn't made her inhibit her ambitions to experience different cultures, but had made her cautious of the placid moments that could give a blow of reality to your romantic dreams.

Alka and Tanya had made her way up to the first-class section of the plane, her dad made sure he had begun the "sending off" process in a big way. All this pampering towards the end of her no longer being his namesake was really sweet. They located their seats, unfortunately, they were on opposite aisles, the drawback of planning a wedding in three months time. She loved to travel with her laid-back, super-funny mom, that loved to try new cuisines as much as she did. The two Varma women were much more experimental and curious about the world than the two grim and austere men of the family. Thank God we were two of each and divided evenly on our personalities. So when they travelled as a family, the men mostly straggled in the vicinity of the hotel rooms, the women were much more adventurous and had to be hunted down at the end of the day by the men in random taxis, yelling at the drivers that hardly understood English. Tanya and Alka were glad that by the time they found them, they're anger had been vented out at the drivers and they were exhausted. Then the next day, the same drill took place, it was pure euphoria.

Tanya sat down at her designated seat and looked out one last time at the bespangled city getting ready to meet obscurity in nightfall. Could a city with such a cyclopian population and so enriched in its resources ever be obscure? Fame and obscurity, albeit, being two sides of the same coin, couldn't really exist without each other, because they define each other, they set the limitations for each other and they never override each other in their importance. Therefore, when fame happens to you, you crave for obscurity so that you can feel normal again, also when obscurity follows fame, you terribly miss the repute. She would really miss Toronto being bathed with the primeval rays of the sun, trying to put up its valorous front for its citizens that had made the city their home and besieging an identity (fame) from it.

She had set off on this amazing journey to find herself and to truly test her limitations. Of what it would be like to be pushed into the most relentless corners of her being, to be ransacked of her inhibitions, only to emerge stronger, wiser and truly gracious about life. Being relentless is your true test of your commitment, being strong is your true test of your righteousness.

She messaged Rohan, confirming him that they boarded the plane as it slowly began to make its ascent towards the sky. The gadgets had to be turned off so that meant you had two means of entertainment to make your journey a pleasant one - make friends with the hemmed in-flight entertainment or make friends with the desolate co-passanger. Tanya didn't have to wait much longer to make that decision, her co-passanger had made that decision for her. "Hi, I am Sonia Antoun. What's your name?" She seemed chirpy, yay for good moods! "I am Tanya. Are you travelling to Delhi?" (the flight had a stopover in Belgium). "Yes. I am originally from Dubai, an architect and a space planner by profession. I am travelling to Delhi for this big collaboration with the popular design firm, Parthav. They are coming up with their own schools attached with recreation centres all over Delhi. Sort of promoting a wholesome and a varied upbringing in kids." She said in one breath. 'That's great! So far had read and heard about Indians being sourced out to the rest of the world, but this is truly refreshing. Great to see India opening its doors to foreign talent. What's the duration of your project?" She asked inquisitively. It was a two-year stint and she had been shortlisted amongst 100 aspiring and talented architects, she had a resume brimming with welfare projects such as old-age homes for senior citizens, hospitals for the ailing and rehabilitation centres for the tussled. Also, what gave her a heads-up was the fact that she was a mom to a little girl, Laila, and knew precisely what was churning in their heads. She very confidently told her that she had envisioned this project with her in mind.

Sonia went onto explaining to her the significance of kids feeling one in the world. With globalization and the infusion of different cultures into their lives via the media, they were imbibing the same values and opinions everywhere. The sector that was the most impacted because of globalization was kids welfare and health, and it was also a sector that needed the most attention. That was because kids were the most impressionable and had to be shaped very delicately. It got Tanya thinking about what these schools would be like. Would they be up by the time she had kids? It was something that her and Rohan were really excited about, having kids. Truly the prime reason for people getting into married life.

She has just met Sonia, but she felt like they had so much in common. Sonia was living the life that she wanted to – to truly be a global citizen and contribute positively to the world. To be able to create a content and favourable environment for the people. They both had high hopes from Delhi, Sonia wanted to bring her dream of creating a healthy environment for kids to life and Tanya wanted to create a meaningful and divine future in country that had called her back after almost 18 years of being away from it. It was also testament to the fact that the length of time wasn't ever a barometer to parade your significance but the magnanimity of your work or dedication towards raising the standards of the world. While, Sonia was only going to be in Delhi temporarily, her work was going to be 'for life'.

Was Tanya ever going to work in Delhi? What had she mapped out for her future to build on her skills? Rohan had asked her to be a housewife, quite sternly so, and it wasn't his fault really. It did seem like it was a bit much to ask from the woman of the present times, but what mattered was her marriage. She was going to put all her resilience and confidence into building a strong marriage, first. That was her priority, for definitely the first five years. She has secretly made up her mind on this. Secondly, she had sworn that she would try to be as in-tune with the women's communities and clubs in Delhi. Thinking along the lines of identity, recognition and fame – she felt that women were bearers of several labels and several titles, that even today child-rearing and household responsibilities (that otherwise go unrecognized) were solely their responsibilities. So even though they had promising and thriving careers, they had to recognize and feel good about managing a home and rearing kids. It was an intricate part of their being, their identities, because you could never put a monetary value on raising a family or nurturing a home. These are roles that enhance your leadership qualities as a woman. In a male-dominated world, it was absolutely important to enhance these qualities. It was impossible to respect, value and admire great women leaders in the future you couldn't identify the areas that make a woman a great leader first. Running a household and making responsible citizens out of your little kids are the best schools to hone such skills. It's free of cost and also very laborious. With this belief, Tanya had put her professional dreams on the back-foot.

She almost swore that if this 'match' had been conceptualized a month later, she would have put her foot down, and been in Paris. She would then put the condition down that he would have to work out of Paris or move to Paris forever. This was a big, big dream of hers. It was one she hadn't given up on, she wanted to run a fashion label one day, named Saisons, so she could make women feel good about themselves, feel good about their bodies, to raise their self-worth in their eyes. She also wished she would have a little, daughter (preferably a first-born), that had her love for styling and fashion, that they would play dressup everyday and that she could pass down her company to her someday. Again, as women, we dream of a world where we have the resources and opportunities to reach our full potential and live free from prejudice and strive for equality rather than dominance. Ideally, Tanya felt that, women were economically empowered when they had financial independence and when they have a voice in the financial decisions to shape their lives and also the lives of their families. Thus women can truly etch their identities when they are socially empowered to have a sense of autonomy, self-confidence, and the power to decide the way they want to steer their private and public lives. When women have the confidence and the means to steer their lives the way they want to, fame isn't too far behind. They can definitely flip the coin on their lives. Fame is a standard that you set out for yourself, that you have achieved and its a true test that you have reached your full potential. One thing to note is that, fame can be transitory but you at your full potential, with your education, your learned skills, your restored faith in yourself is forever. Often you get the best chance to hone yourself in obscurity, because it demands your 100% focus. You have to forget everything else, it is your cynosure and you fuel your life with your undivided attention and energies. So even in obscurity, you are a star waiting to be born or re-born.

CHAPTER 8

We got off at the Brussles, Belgium airport for a quick breakfast, cuz for two hungry women eating omlette and toast on the flight could happen everyday, but a crisp Pelmini followed by some waffles topped with nutella was a rarity. It was like wearing an Akoya pearl necklace instead of your usual corals, like wearing a Balmain mini instead of a Mango mini, it was strutting about in Manolos instead of Nine Wests. Appraising yourself to life's little scarcities didn't just give you a thrill that you were alive, but also made you realize that if you could acquire these rarities, then you were living the good life. That you hadn't stagnated and although materialistic things aren't ever known to be the fillers for burrows left by unfulfilled goals, but they can certainly give you the much necessary boost to regroup yourself and resurrect those goals.

Airports often accelerated those stagnated goals. Many reasons for it. Firstly, airports never ceased from functioning, when Tanya looked around, she saw a-lot of movement. People hastening to board their flights, porters rallying around passengers to make smooth transitions and the mess continually disposing off appetizing smells to keep you even more alert and aware of your surroundings. Also, when you board a plane, the abyss between earth and air (two elements necessary for survival) disappears. When in flight, you defy gravity, you become unsinkable and you become celestial, almost superhuman. A century ago, this wouldn't have been possible. So then this testament to the fact that despite the defeats or the unfulfilled goals, life moves on. That moving ahead, one step at a time, was the way to go. As she took a nibble at the waffle after a delish meal, she felt resurrected from her anxieties of starting married life. Reputed to be a very important phase in people's life, rightly so, because you procreate. So after she shopped for a Guess bag for herself and a Coco Chanel perfume, she felt so charged up. She changed into a kurta, trousers and sandals from her skinny jeans, top and shoes – transitioning you see! She suddenly became excited to meet her new family, the Delhiites – known for their enormous hearts and appetites also.

The last leg of the journey was kind of upbeat. Tanya very curiously began chatting with Sonia, as she broke out with her floor plans, fraught with goodies for little kids. From a soccer field adjoining from the back of a school to an 11-feet swimming pool in the community centre to a library stacked with encyclopedias, journals and magazines from around the world, she almost felt so positive and hopeful about her future. Ofcourse, when two women begin to chat, topics such as fashion, shoes and light-bashing about co-passengers (often called gossip) aren't to be missed. Tanya was never a fan of the in-flight entertainment, not even when her favourite heroes such as George Clooney or Ryan Reynold's movies were featured. Nope! People and their animated expressions (possibly because of the drinks and then being confined to their seats coupled with excitement of going to meet their loved ones) were much more fun. It was more spontaneous and exciting than planning an impromptu clubbing night on a Wednesday in university when you had a 5.30 am case-study the next day.

The flight began to descent towards Delhi. An amazing sight to savour! It was just before afternoon. So while in Toronto, the moon had begun to display its allurement, trying to sendoff the city into a lovely tailspin, the sun in Delhi was cascading its glory to get its citizens to gleefully tread-on with their stints. The flight-attendant was making her customary announcement. That also seemed like music, like a part of your experience. For Tanya, this wasn't just some ordinary journey. It was a life-changing one. One that would shape her personality, one that would add tiers to her wisdom, one that would hopefully shed her of her inhibitions and make her a bit more street-smart of people. It was much like those

balance sheets with contrasting numbers (that didn't have any connections) and varying values that needed to be aligned so that they could be of some benefit. So, starting from that very moment, she had to add tiers of meaning to her life.

CHAPTER 9

W hen approaching such a life-change, it's good to always take a step back and gage the responses of the new people in your life, just so you don't come off as too overbearing and too irrational. So instead of hoping around the airport, it was good to be the 'statue' that she would be reputed to be in the next nine years of her life. The gates of the flight had been unbolted and as she stepped out, she was firstly greeted by the broiling winds that jolted your muscles from the long journey, almost 3/4 around the globe, and so you were kind of sore anyway. Also, you hadn't slept for the last 11 hours, so then you didn't want to break-out into a Zumba session either. Mom's instructions were to be absolutely silent and still, more silent and still than being at mass on a Sunday at 'Duomo Di Milano' in Milan, Italy. Even though you are completely enamoured with the grandeur of the place, the gracefulness displayed by the pink-hued marbles its built with and its significance to the people of **Milan**, you can't help but be respectful to the message behind it – that by being silent you are being respectful to others, that you aren't forgetting them in your prayers and that it truly takes a village for you to exist. Thus, by being quiet and letting her new family make the first moves of introductions, she was being respectful to the moment and to the curious and anxious people in Rohan's life, that she wasn't ever going to be more significant to him than any of them, be it his distant cousins or his juniors in office that had like a one-month stint in his office. That she would want them to have an opinion in his life and that their opinions would be valued, by him, even if she wasn't coherent with them. Her significance would be decided by them as a couple and the boundaries would be set by him and him only. She knew she would be happy in that designated space because she was his wife, his co-partner that would help him steer his life in the right direction. Being a wife is quite a position of prestige, she had seen her mom portray that position with much pride and happiness. You get to be a part of all of your husband's dreams, you get to watch him work endless hours, slog towards giving you and your family all the comforts of life, its a kick to watch! You get the best seats in the house, its like centre-court during the playoffs. You get to seize time when your team wins the trophy.

Also Tanya, chuckled as she spotted Rohan standing from afar, because he seemed quite nervous. More nervous when Kobe hit a short one within 24 seconds of the finishing of the game (from past Bruce Bowen) during the 2008 playoffs. She tried to "strutt whatever you call it" walking towards him, pure immaturity and trying too hard to follow J-LO, as she walked towards him. She was able to hook his eyes on her, fully thinking, that he would be humming that song "moves" like Mick Jagger by Maroon 5, as he scoured this trifle of a woman he was about to marry. Then, she actually realized that he was staring at this tag that kind of beetling around her carry-on wandering if she would trip. Waste of a walk, waste of 30 bucks of Nine-West shoes that would synchronize her legs in a way that would fine-tune his eyes and then waste of hours and hours of conceptualizing this moment when he would first see her. The kid was more worried if I was gonna trip and fall, might as well have, at-least he would run to rescue me from this downer of a moment. He began to walk towards her, holding his baby-niece in his arms, probably propped on his lap by his doting elder brother, in hopes of fatherhood. When he finally firmed his eyes on her, he strapped out this relived smile of his as he could sense she was a cool as a cucumber, giggling because she realized why Ayushi (all of five months old) was planted in his arms as she was squirming like a little rabbit actually. She gave him a hug, then heard him say a gentle "hi". Then she spotted his parents right behind. She snatched his attention to them and touched their feet. Then his sister-in-law was right behind, followed by his brother-in-law. It was great to have them all at the airport. That moment, for Tanya, was very reassuring, that they were going to be around for her.

Her mom wasn't too far behind, but was quite nervous about the introductions and specially after this super-long flight. She had raised her kids with utmost care and she was one of those women that really prided on her family. So, handing over the reigns (reigns = nurturing) of her daughter's life in Rohan's hands was a bit on the skittish side. It wasn't cuz she wanted to be the 'final say' in the way she ran her life, that wasn't ever the case. But, that Tanya was stepping into married life. It kind of reminded Tanya of the time when Greg Popovich (he loved it when we called him Big Poppa for sure),coach of her favourite team basketball team -Spurs, took over the responsibility from Bob Hill back in 1996, after the team had begun the season with a 3-18 streak. Plagued with injuries that turned into apprehensions about the team's game, Popovich stepped in to make history. He made stars out of Manu Ginobbli, Tony Parker, Tim Duncan and ofcourse Shaquille O'Neil. His ability to maneuver pieces to the benefit of team became his forte. Surely, the appointing of coaches in basketball can be seen as a business-decision rather than anything else, but the chemistry between team-players, the intent to actually execute mean tactics such as the 'intentional foul play' or the forming of the 'forward circle' (that only made sense from the top-most seats and you weren't intoxicated) required some gusto, an innate sense of desire to win. These very skills could never be quantified or pre-determined. Similarly, to steer a marriage in the right direction, there needs to be some confidence and trust between the couple. Tanya's mom was just in a way looking for that nod of assurance from Rohan. Rohan and Tanya were sitting in the lounge area, conversating like long-lost friends, reunited after ages. Rohan immediately took over the reigns, his strategy was effective communication and that you would be ensured of a good time if you co-operated in the major decisions.

Also, arranged marriages are criticized for the same reason, that they are conceptualized because people of the same social-standing in society want to maintain it and want a similar kind of lifestyle and values to be passed down to their future generations. It seems really financially-sparked but its double the work and effort because you carry-on the hopes of your respective families and the social circle that you belong to. The most successful marriages, that are arranged marriages, are built from very strong and staunch values, which works to the benefit of the couple eventually – they are financially, emotionally and socially better off as a team, its all about having the will to make it work. Teamwork in a marriage takes time to show its benefits, initially, one person out of the couple, has to take the lead get this "courtship" to sail. Due to the submissive and laid-back nature of Tanya, she was only pro-active at work, Alka felt like Rohan was best suited for her as he was more the "take the bull by the horns" kind of person. She no longer felt the pressure to nudge Tanya to "get her act together and get things in order", someone was going to do it for her.

Tanya was led out by Rohan in a separate car, he drove her around for a bit until they all met at his house. Tanya was at complete ease, she felt assured in his company, the only thing that was kind of giving her the jitters were this wedding that was going to happen in a month's time. It was amazing that they were both so calm and excited about this rather than being all "what's gonna happen" to us in five years. You should never think so far ahead, never. Because the world around isn't going to be the same in five years, you will be required to change, that is definite. To what degree, you can never predict, so why think so far ahead? Ask a Vince Carter or a Lebron James when they were new to the game and signed onto new teams, a double task of sorts, but changed the destiny of the sport and their individual careers by adhering to win-win strategies and accepting the changes in the game as the seasons passed by. So a new marriage with a new person is double task of sorts, but you have to think win-win. Unlike basketball, you can't make off-season shuffles or you can't really "grade" your beloved on this pre-determined, standard ranking system, but you can always make it up with expensive gifts and lots of good communication. Success is a possibility, it just requires "more bounce than the ounce".

CHAPTER 10

It was a blazing June-afternoon in Delhi, all of 10 days after they had landed, and the families had gathered at Tanya's aunt Nisha and uncle Bikram's place for the "Roka" ceremony. Might have been a droughty and a semi-baked (weather-wise) afternoon outside, but it sure was joyous and chipper indoors. Quick fact on the way "progress" is locked-down in a relationship amongst Indian families, is to have a quick "roka" ceremony with a priest, family members and a dhol (for wedding songs). The ceremony consists of exchanging rings, performing a little prayer and then getting small gifts from family members, all well-documented in pictures, so that the formalizing process could be validated.

With the wedding just a month away, this could have happened the next day but it took 10 days because Tanya got bit by the flu bug, it wasn't because this just happened to people living in Delhi, its cuz she belly-floped right onto having "barf ka golaas" (flavored ice on a stick) like twice everyday. Then her belly began to flip flop its way into fever-land. Doctors after doctors were referred to because the bride-to-be can't be bed-ridden like leading up-to a wedding. She has people to visit, outfits to finalise and dances to learn, she certainly can't make mistakes in her dances, its like her demo that she presents to the groom's family. She was on some five-day antibiotics dose but it had gotten the best of her immunity. It was also a strong indicator of what she was to expect, she was cautioned.

So the Roka began first with Rohan sitting-in for the prayers in the living room. As the priest began his chants, the family members broke into songs in the background, one that Tanya could make-out was called "banno teri akhiyan" (complementing the bride on her eyes). Soon, Tanya was beckoned into the living room, she was wearing this royal-blue, light chiffon-saree with a deep-cut (from the back) blouse. She sat down beside him and then began the "proper" part of the ceremony. Tanya got her first "culture shock" as she had to repeat the prayers with chaste Hindi words, only to be egged-on with giggles from the ladies. Then, Rohan stepped in to help her, but it was only to help smoothen things so that the sighs and giggles could stop. This was going to be one of the many firsts, where she would be tested on her "Indianess". Really, if you thought brushing-up on all your standard prayers, hymns and recipes for all the "prasads" would get you many browny-points, then you were mistaken. This was all just amateur stuff, like Tanya's dad called it the "technician" of all the IT professionals. To get some respectability in being a good-Indian, wife you needed to maintain a good house, maintain your health, have well-mannered kids and display as many dishes as you could at your dinner-parties. She had a long road ahead of her, she was determined though. To be a good Indian wife is an uphill battle, but the rewards are plenty. Smiling faces and knowing that you believe in win-win. So, while she was barely managing her way into saying the lines properly, one of the family members began singing the "sheher ki ladkiyon ke peeche" from the movie JO Jeeta Wohi Sikander. Translation = Guys that run after girls brought up in cities don't realize the allurement that exists in women from small towns. To which Rohan squeeled out a "Main sab seekha doonga" (I'll teach her everything). It was as assuring as the Indian post offices promising that your Rakhis would reach on-time, but they don't ever.

Before they knew it, the ceremony had ended, and thankfully, so did the songs. They were no longer just in a courtship, but the Miss Congeniality contest had just begun.   Tanya then got up, got the blessings of the elders in the family and was smiling ear-to-ear. Truly, you can have all the degrees in the world, but the "crown jewels" of appreciation of aunties in the Indian societies only is acquired when you've built a happy home.

She began to serve lunch to all the guests, and then got into sort of a survey of questions on her skills, about the number of cuisines she had specialized in, that if she wanted to lose the extra 5 pounds then had she looked into the 'Mediterranean Diet'? Also, what were her strategies to manage her work and her personal life together? She was referred to atleast 5 dieticians, 5 yoga centres, 5 placement agencies and then also tips on what to wear for the wedding. Such a 'tiramisu' moment after an 'all you can eat Chinese buffet on Chinese New Year' meal. Like when Kate is swept away by the waves and Jack saves her in the end in Titanic! Like when Raj lands up in India to rescue Simran from a disdainful of a man in Dilwale Dulhaniya Le Jayenge! Like when a distraught Meghna comes back from a serious downfall in her career for that triumphant walk, displaying great confidence in Fashion! The support system that were going to test her abilities as she walked the thin line of rope between balancing and revelling in her duties, were actually going to be her saviours in life. There was no need to feel intimidated at all.

"Beta, serve these snacks, one by one, to everyone. Start with these sandwiches." Her mom called out to her. It was time to exercize, and simultaneously display, the crisp and perfect hostess skills.

She truly felt like she was in a circus, walking the thin rope of expectations (meaning delish snacks, smiling, dressed immaculately, guests basking in the ambience of exotic scents in the house, dim lights, great music) and reality (nervous about - snacks being too cold, anxiously grinning, the buttons of your blouse popping out, the chandelier being too bright and drifty music). Nonetheless, she was up for it.

She could sense Rohan's gaze anchored at her as she served everyone, conversated with his family members and tried to appreciate the fact that she was chosen to be a part of them. At times, he would hop into her conversations to make sure she didn't feel too out of place, which she didn't. What was going to happen when he would be busy at work, all day, then she knew she could count on them, might as well blend in! Mr Mathur, his life, him being a lawyer, living and working in Delhi (one of world's busiest cities, with regards to traffic) and being very attached and considerate towards his college-friends were his choices. Tanya was going to marry the man, his life, she had no qualms about fitting-into everyone's likes and dislikes. He seemed more anxious than her, she was acting like she had been put on this inciting and thrilling roller-coaster and actually had to be jolted, several times, to wake up from her fantasy. When you take-on such a big life-change, you are serious about it, just the lead upto the wedding day is kind of a big high. You want to be dazed, you want to be intoxicated in all this love and acceptance. Screw reality! Sometimes, that is! It's absolutely normal to be separated from reality, for a little while, because it emancipates you from the gravity of your worries and it can often weigh you down from reaching towards growth. There isn't any need to worry, these quickies, or rather, moments of escapism don't last long. The worries, in form of distractions, manage to seep into your escapism because there isn't a way to minimize your pain but to face life head-on.

Before Tanya knew it, she was back into bouts of sneezing, and the party was about to end. They had been given the task to finalize the guest-list, work-out the trips to the markets and also finalize their outfits for the ceremonies. Tanya had been given a few whispers on the fact that Rohan wasn't keen on wearing sherwanis. They finally managed to have a sit down, but the task wasn't as achievable as they had thought. They were given these long lists to stream-line. Which guests to be placed for the vegetarian meals because their religious sentiments had to be respected and which guests had to be specially invited for the "happy hours" in the evenings because you wanted them to have a "swell time" and which guests to line-up for the dances for the Sangeet because they were excited for you. Rohan stressed on the fact that each and every guest had to be entertained to the hilt, because each of their presence meant the world to him. Tanya, as always, was more practical. She felt that cutting-costs by grouping people would be more manageable. She started each conversation with, "Get family A,B,G and K to stay on the left wing because they have small kids and the pool and park are close by" or "Group Nana, Dadima, Bua-Dadis and Mausi-Nanis together on the ground floor because it was accessible by wheel-chairs" or "Get the dancers for Sangeet on the third floor because all that noise from the music won't bother anybody". Rohan was kind of perplexed at the enormity of such an event, this certainly didn't happen just a generation before them. Where Tanya had already started to forge strategies of managing such a big group of people for a three-day event, Rohan wanted things to be more random and spontaneous. He kept interrupting on her suggestions because grouping people restricted the flow, the energy and communication amongst them. Each and every person had the right to experience everything at the resort and that grouping them would be like curbing their experience. Weddings, specially Indian weddings, were a vital, reliable and esteemed source of networking for Indian families, so with this traditional view, Rohan was keen to restrict from grouping people. This was one of the first junctures of conflict between the two, Rohan often stood by his traditional views because he was brought up traditionally, Tanya had more of a practical, world-ly view of things, You really can't live in the West if you aren't practical with your cost and with your 'peeps'. Despite the fact that weddings still managed to retain that charm and sanctity from previous generations, today, it was all about 'the experience'. To provide a sort of 'wholesome entertainment' for people to remember and because families are generally scattered all over the world, it was a time for them to truly rejoice and relish every moment possible with your loved-ones. If you were to hire professional wedding-planners, then, they tend follow the same mantra as do the producers and directors of 'Blockbuster Entertainers' of present times. These movies promote luxurious lifestyles, with the best things, best of education, stylish clothes, foreign actresses to throw in that bit of exotica, remixing their music to widen their base and commuting via helicopters to reduce distances (to say the least).

Basically, to provide escapism in that three-hour window of opportunity they get. The producer, while packaging the film, hires the crew for the film – right from the director to the stylists, so while they are keen on the script (the basis on which each film is built, the true moneymaker), they try to decorate it with as much froth so that it appeals to all your senses and that it has you hooked for life. Weddings, these days, were no different. With a constant flow of entertainment, cuisines and theme-based activities, all your senses were tapped into and you were stimulated to the best of your abilities.

These experiences are forever etched in your memory as moments you can always relate to when you want to escape from the matters of contention in your life. The sojourn from reality to fantasy, irrespective of the time-frame, is like the build-up towards an awakening towards the impossible things in life. Movies such as Superman taught you to fly, Ajooba educated you on the ways to conquer a kingdom, Koi Mil Gaya taught you to overcome your shortcomings and Mr India taught you to disappear in order to win over the evil. Weddings taught you to pledge your love for the person that has helped you in your most difficult times, in the presence of God, which meant that some celestial presence is necessary for you to symbolize the most significant event of your life. It was truly going to be a time when Tanya felt like she could rise above all material things and embrace this big step in her life.

CHAPTER 11

Before Tanya and her family got their heads wrapped around the scale of this wedding, there was all this shopping to be done. The Varma's (Tanya's family) and the Mathurs (Rohan's family) had this ginormous task of carrying out this event of sorts in a very smooth and orderly manner. Yet there was no end to their joy. Anil, Tanya's father, had arrived to make this chaotic circus of flaring tempers, differing opinions, endless drinking sessions, complete. The 'mithaiwalla' was making fifteen extra dabbas, which had Vikram uncle upset, the 'tentwallas' had sourced the wrong colour for the Sangeet ceremony (florescent blue instead of florescent pink) which made Tanya's dad livid and when the Jaipur tourism people called to say that they could only book 10 taxis instead of 15, the entire family was ready almost ready to serve the wedding-planning agency a mean notice, this was the show of their lives, they had to impress. The incharge of this entire event was to be stationed at 'Jag Mandir' palace hotel in Jaipur, immediately, but he went missing. His name was Rahul Sinha and he pretended like he was more in control of this entire situation than PM Wilfred Laurier was during the cultural revolution

and wanted to protect key industries, more stern about his convictions than PM Lester B Pearson was during the signing of the NATO treaty and more tolerant of differing opinions and cultures than PM Trudeau had displayed to be. Jaipur was under the radar, it had become more reputable than Capitol Hill. Tanya, being the only sane character at that moment, decided to play the role of Peter Jennings (world-famous Canadian News Correspondent), and sort of grab the bull by the horns.

(NOTE TO EDITOR: CAN I MENTION TRUDEAU EVEN THOUGH HE WAS ELECTED AFTER THIS PROPOSED MARRIAGE TOOK PLACE IN 2009)

She called up his 'private number' and he answered by saying, "Ahaa Kalyanam Wedding Planners (translation = Wow Marriage), myself Rahul Sinha, can I help you?" Tanya replied even before he finished his sentence, "This is Tanya Varma, I'm calling regarding the Varma-Mathur wedding that's to take place next month. Alot of stuff has been stalled because of it, there's alot of repetition from other weddings and there aren't enough taxis to transport people in and out of Jaipur. Also, the total costing of this entire wedding hasn't been finalised and we can see why! What's really the matter?" He, as much in a hurry replied by saying, "how can we finalise the entire wedding a whole month prior Tanyaji? Yahan to sabkuch shaadi ke roz finalise hota hay, Tanyaji" Tanya was aghast! Being in finance, the very first rule of number-crunching was violated, which was, to have your numbers ready before you execute your plans! Where were the actuals? The projected numbers? and the worst case scenarios also had to be accounted for. What was he talking about? Her faint-hearted family couldn't take-on this last-minute encumbrance of a task of handling money. Certainly not when the traffic of relatives swinging in and out of the venue would be in large numbers.

She tried to make Rahul see eye-to-eye with the way he was winging it big time, she wanted him to come back to reality on things. How ironic, when she could barely keep her feet on the ground from excitement. She spoke with some sort of assertiveness, saying, "Rahulji, ye sab cheez aap hame abhi finalise kar ke do within one week's time. Please I request ki aap abhi ya to Delhi aayee ya mujhe ek update within tomorrow night bhejeeye." Rahul Sinha paused for a bit, in Jaipur he was feasting and drinking like 'dem kings because he was "sampling" you see, but in Delhi he would have to straight-up be on the job, get things done and spend his own money while he was commuting from end of the place to another. So, then he manages the reply, "Tanyaji, aap kham a kha pareshaan ho rahi hain, aapko kya update chahiye?"

So, she had her laptop open and she quickly opened up a fresh Microsoft-excel sheet and jotted down the variables (food, decorations, transportation) on one side and the timeline for each as the constant (a very basic update sheet for analysis). At the same time, she kept conversating with him and then also had him list all the vendors. Things weren't that un-systematic from the West, wedding planners, no matter where, wanted people to have a good time, but in India, one very key characteristic that they possessed was that they had an excuse for every delayed aspect, and they validated it too, so then there were no arguments. You just had to accept it, put your money where their mouth was. Because that was the only way to get things done. Period. As Tanya began with the very first updates of each of the variables, and then appeared all the excuses. "Krystal crockeries are expecting a shipment for your colors in two weeks so we need to wait until the full inventory is here unless we give them some extra cash to speed it up. Because of the rising fuel prices, Vansh taxis have reduced their number of cars and its also summer plus off-season plus they are also relocating so we might have to (not need to) give them some extra cash to increase their fleet. Ronak tentwallas are overbooked with two more weddings that very weekend so your theme and colors are being repeated unless we give them extra cash and you can first dibbs on your choice." He said, very confidently. Tanya got the whiff of exactly how business was done and that her dream wedding was taking all the fantasy elements off of it. No wonder, word of mouth, held no meaning where money was the only substantial and relevant factor in closing deals.

The next three weeks, she realised, that her lessons in real-world had been realized. She was so accustomed to the value of work and research put behind calculated numbers on these meticulously formatted excel sheets, they had such integrity to them. No matter the scale of the assignment you were given. Was the real world ever like this? Didn't the vendors feel that having strong actuals from previous weddings were the best form of communication for their businesses, didn't the middle-men feel that their USP factor would be more appealing if it was based on concrete and consistent numbers rather than seasonal and economically-driven. She felt a bit let-down, that she had managed to handle quite a few key projects in an impressive manner at work. One of them being managing the financials of an entire channel for Canada's premiere broadcasting company. Why did her own wedding seem so tedious and sapping, when this was going to be the biggest high of her life?

She turned to her father for help. He was really trying to empathize with her, but was actually laughing inside. It's like that time when you first learn to play chess from your daddy and then try to defeat them at their own mastery, and each time you lose, they laugh because its like the training wheels shrieking to come off but it isn't time yet. Similarly, it wasn't time yet for Tanya to understand the sensibilities of people working in a new country, but his silent guidance had already begun. He had nudged her to take-up the scouting and curbing of the expenses so that she could understand the 'human aspects' of conducting a business. Till date, she was in service, so her soft skills were kind of dormant, she was only evaluated and appraised based on her mathematical skills, which meant being pretty much behind the scenes. But her father had created this awareness in her that caning out the same contents of skills by creating spreadsheets for everything, didn't work under every scenario (the only next time when it would make sense was when she was charting her kid's sleeping and feeding schedule, more of that later). He asked her to call Rahul again and be more interpersonal with him. She called him up, and then, spoke to him with much warmth, saying "Rahulji, sorry I was very rude before, its just that I'm used to handling things differently, aapke hisaab se, agar hum saare vendors ek request karein, ki agar woh hamare saare conditions pure karein to hum unhe Sangeet ke din dinner and drinks ke liye invite kar sakte hain (with one guest) , where they get to do some networking and can revel in the music and ambience that they have helped create. You are also invited, we'll set up a special table right by the stage so that they get a chance to come up and address the guests. Instead of extra cash, it would be more obligatory of us." Rahul instantly said yes. Her father wanted to get up and applaud her, but instead he chugged down his drink and gave her a hug. Out of his two kids, Tanya needed to be nudged a bit more because much more was expected of her. The younger one, being a boy, was just expected to follow by examples set by his elder sister. Tanya's parents always focused on her a bit more (she hated to admit, but it was so evident to their family and friends) because Ayaan had the front-row seat while she was being experimented on. Before they knew it, he at the age of 18, had become as much sensible, independent wrt his thoughts, considerate towards others and delightful to be in company of, as much as his sister. It was a family joke, that they hardly knew he existed until Tanya had left for university and they just began to ponder around his room because the house was painfully quiet.

Ayaan was an expert at developing and exercising his soft skills, because that's precisely the way you get to hog the limelight from an elder sibling that is more of a mystery than an exhibit at the Royal British Colombia Museum and is only prominent because she is the older sibling, hence being dated in comparison.

Her uncles and father were about to sit-down for some Thai food and drinks, a usual routine for when the family got-together. Rohan had just called. He was coming to pick her up for dinner, he was busy mugging up for these exams that were to be written like a week prior to the wedding. He needed a break, so he called her up and asked her in a more straight up manner, "you busy or what?" To which she replied, "nope, what's up?" "I need a break from all this memorizing, my mind is about to burst from all this knowledge and I won't really need like 35% of it ever. Theory is such a waste. Be ready in like 30." He added. "Ok!" Such "straightupness", if there is a word, was the first of many, many impromptu plans that he would make and just expect her to be ready and chirpy just because he needed a break from a hectic work-day. So much for soft-skills and their effectiveness, if you can't really exercise them on like your significant other. She was like psssh! She was okay for the ride, he needed to vent out his anxieties, and she was keen on knowing why. She genuinely felt like she could help him ease the stress in his work, but a more romantic way of addressing their date would have been nicer. It was okay anyway, the kid was busier than a dyke in a hardware store. So, she was his shock-absorber in a way that was refreshing for him. You can never expect a constant flow of romantic phrases or raging hormones that would lead to many sexual escapades, there's your Jane Austen for that, but you have to be the carrier of these soft-skills. Calm them down when they worry too much, talk to them in details and delve into the causes of concern in their worries.

Having stellar soft-skills is a true test of your character. There can't be any deadlines in love. There can't be any grey areas when you're in love, you have to balance out. You have to be just as much of an asset to him than a liability. The one drawback of analysts is that they swear by repetition and redundancy. Any trend that gives them the slightest hint that they're numbers are deviating and won't ever make sense, they eliminate it, immediately. If it can't be eliminated then there's an entire set of tools to analyse this trend. Then they close it forever. Never to be mentioned again. Basically repetition works because you just have to adhere to allocated policies and schedule requirements. Redundancy in a relationship just squeezes the excitement out of it, it just makes your loved-one too accustomed to what to expect. Thus, the way you manage your relationship through the ups and downs gives strength and genuineness to your character.

From relation experts like Dr Phil to Kareena in her movies encourage you to 'Switch it Up" with your significant other because serious emotions are at stake. The emotional experience of boredom or missing your loved one just makes it all-the-more impossible to ignore them and reach-out to them in different ways, so you can maintain that gaze that got hooked onto you when the ship your love-affair first sailed. What was Tanya going to do differently for this dinner-date, wear a black saree, that would totally get his attention, he had mentioned it once, but she hadn't worn it since. She was being considerate towards him.

Unlike her work-profile, she couldn't ever eliminate feelings of missing him like a wayward trend, she was quite jubilant that he was turning to her as she was his safe-harbour.

CHAPTER 12

For beautiful eyes, look for the good in others; for beautiful lips, speak only words of kindness; and for poise, walk with the knowledge that you are never alone." - Audrey Hepburn

Tanya's big wedding weekend had arrived, and extravagantly so. Audrey Hepburn was an idol for Tanya and she had sort of made this quote her mantra for life. Style, in form of clothes that makes

you look good, makes so much sense. When, dressed in best garbs, you get a chance to enhance your personality, they are like unspoken words that convey alot about your mindset, your respect for your body.

Jag Mandir palace was overflowing with jubilant people, radiating with different arrays of music and glistening in the aura of two families celebrating a great union in presence of God. Alot of efforts and thoughts had gone into making this event a memorable one, guests were eagerly awaiting to delve into the many goodies that were ready to stimulate their various senses and awaken a sense of familiarity and nostalgia that they didn't usually get to see in the hustle of their own lives. The most anticipated aspect of the wedding was Tanya's outfits. Was she just as excited to showcase her picks for the day that would change her life forever?

Her clothes weren't only part of this sensory overload, but they actually were like the "showstoppers" of a designer's collection that they design with their most sincere and earnest efforts. Style on your wedding day is so discrepant from style on your regular days, it has to be because of its significance to your life, its significance to the way you feel about your beloved and its significance in the way you want to present yourself to the world as his Mrs.

"These strings are quite delicate Tanya di, they might break-open any minute if you stretch too much or lapidate your arms into a 'Vinyasa Yoga Aasana," squirmed Darsha, her nervous little cousin sister. "You got them done in a size too small, you should have stretched them out to be at least an inch or two wider!" She sounded very reaffirming as she managed to tie them up and bring some composure to the blouse of her saree. "Why do we choose such complicated outfits for our weddings? When we have many more things to do, more importantly dance to our hearts-content!" "True. Its such a conflicting feeling, the lead upto your wedding is like all about your flashy outfits, but when your wedding happens, you just can't wait to get them off and get into your chappals and shorts! I know I'm never going to wear these clothes again, feels like such a waste. Have I already climaxed in in this entire furor about what am I going to wear?"

"All brides-to-be climax like a minute before they get into their outfits, di, because their feelings and the wedding itself becomes more significant than these garbs, its just the face of your beloved that you want to see. Its just all the noise, the atmosphere, that makes these clothes feel so unimportant. Only in pictures do they make sense after." She wasn't preaching, she was absolutely right. She, herself was wearing this magenta, brocade saree with beaded-work on it and was barely able to walk like a feet in them."

This was her wedding night, and her scarlett-red saree with intricate bronzed-embroidery work was very traditional, reminiscent of the bright red colors exhibited by designers all over the world in the 90s in excitement and hopes for a unified and progressive century ahead. While finalizing her saree, she remembered a very enticing quote by designer Yves St Laurent, ""The most beautiful accessory for a woman is a passion for fashion. But cosmetics are easier to buy." What better day to exercise this passion than your wedding day, though?" She thought, as she was left alone in the room when her cousin sisters went out to welcome the Baraat. The harmonious succession of songs played by the band as the baraat was led in made her realize that the process of a wedding was serious stuff. If you

were the bride, the most important person in this event, then you had to display your best facets so that you could double your excitement, and her passion for fashion was exactly what she wanted to bring into focus. It was to truly make people realize that she had aligned her emotions with her understanding of the relevance of occasion.

When she saw Rohan, dressed in his cream sherwani, stationed at the stage, upraised about three feet above the spectators, she realized that the blush on her cheeks would definitely align with the blush-red color of her saree as she was also hoisted in status from a Ms to a Mrs. That was the point she was trying to make, that is precisely the point every fashion designer wants to make with their statement pieces, that style isn't just an accessory, it is a feeling that can be paralleled with your life to make it more meaningful.

Soon, she was beckoned by her cousin sisters, from like three doors down the hallway, to get set for her Doli. She was lead into the open-air by them and one look around and she was bewildered to see this sea of assorted colours in form of garbs worn by people. From the leafy greens to the shimmering aubergines to the dreamy aquamarines, it just felt like one big concert with psychedelic lamps and bands floating amongst the dusky hours. It was like she was back in the 90s, yes those very hopeful and optimistic 90s, when she was lifted up by these grade 12 boys from the boroughs (the non-prissy ones) during a Backstreet Boys Concert at Air Canada Centre and these very colors were decorating the ambience with their luminosity and charm. Then it was the experience of a new cultural revolution that brought together every teenager like her in the world on the same level of understanding as her, today, it was the experience of an age-old tradition that aligned her with every other woman that pledged her love to her significant other. Two very poignant events, but very satiating in fulfilling her desires, at different stages in her life. Famous designer Vivienne Westwood, very aptly put it that, "Fashion is very important. It is life-enhancing and, like everything that gives pleasure, it is worth doing well." Thus, for Tanya, that lived and breathed fashion, was able to conceptualize this outfit and make it her own because she had envisioned the significance of this night. The sporadic twinkling of flashes of cameras and phones gave her the reassurance that she had made the right choice of an outfit that would be become quite iconic for her.

When she reached the stage, Rohan's face was radiating more than all the bling put together by all the women in the crowds. She was hoping for a very comforting comment, and aptly so, he mouthed out a "wow! You look stunning." and she might as well have dived into the crowds screaming, "I envisioned it...err...I want it that way." (a song sung by BSB). She then was able to let lose and truly revel in the moment. They were handed garlands made of fresh cabbage-roses, strong in their fragrance but very pleasing to the eyes. Tanya was truly enveloped in the moment, the music, the ambience, the fountains of champagne gently oozing into everyone's spirits, making them as much energetic and fascinated with two people, sitting stoicly, just gazing at them as they tried to entertain the spectators with their smiles and waves. They were sort of performers in a way, entertaining, pleasing, making music with their gazes and the way they stole moments of tender conversations with each other. Truly, there isn't a way to please your spectators but to feel good about yourself first, be confident in your decisions and in your intentions. No wonder, successful artists, specially designers, are so popular with their crafts, because they're so confident in themselves and their craft. Only when you are confident in accepting your flaws and enhancing your strengths, can you gain the confidence of others. Another lesson to learn from them, that beauty and goodwill comes from within.

So, from a very fussy and ostentatious outfit, Tanya changed into into a chastened and a conventional one. A traditional Bihari, yellow saree with a golden zari border and a pink, Jaipuri dupatta with gold bootas on it. Yellow sarees are traditionally worn for the actual wedding ceremony. A staple outfit, colors and texture to make the ceremony truly more about the vows than about the outfits or the bride for that matter. As Coco Chanel very aptly put it, "Fashion changes, but style endures." When the really frothy elements of a wedding wear you out, the drinking, dancing, endless, gossipy conversations and the bullying of the younger cousins, you crave for some simplicity. Fashion is temporary, style is permanent. Fashion is ever-changing, style is constant because its your instinct. Fashion is very experimental, but style demands perfect proportions. Thus, for Tanya, her outfits didn't only exhibit the undertones of evolving fashion trends of Indians, but it also gave a nod to an age-old tradition, thus proving that style prevails over fashion.

After like, watching the bride and groom gyrate, spin and pirouette like those models on the runways, with as much grace and thrill, showcasing the most sleek clothes, its really very refreshing to have them focus on the relevance and sanctity of the wedding ceremony. Suddenly, all the chaos of the wedding festivities amasses into this one place, where God presides and us mortals embrace his benevolence.

Tanya had danced her heart out at the Ladies Sangeet in her flashy peach-lehenga, gotten her simple white saree blotched with the auspicious yellow colour for the 'haldee' and swooned everyone with her romantic red number for the 'jaimaal', but actually got everyone's undivided attention at her wedding ceremony. She was led in by Shweta and Darsha, her little cousin sisters, into this mandap decorated with white Lillies and Eden roses. The canope was brisk enough to shadow the couple from the gashing rays of the sun, only the sounds of the chants and hymns were to be heard, along with the spectators singing traditional weddings songs to enhance the importance of the ambience. The slight nip in the air, despite it being a June wedding, was also jolting in a way to reawaken you from your slumber, induced by the long hours of partying.

"Didi, hold your pleats as you walk upto the mandap" whispered a concerned Shweta, as she helped Tanya get upto her chair. Tanya, very consciously, or rather heedlessly, made it up to her seat, and sat beside Rohan. Her little sisters sat right behind her to make sure she was supplied with everything she needed. The ceremony began with the priest saying a short prayer, then commencing with the chants. "Such a relief, from the blaring speakers to this noble priest, solemnizing and summarizing the entire event together."

Tanya heard her sisters talk. Everyone seemed to be on like this detox from having all their senses worked out.

In the midst of the ceremony, Tanya peered out of her translucent ghoonghat, and spotted some peculiar elements that were common at everyone's wedding, her aunt Reena was flipping through the pages of the a little read-along book to keep up with the priest, her cousins Anamika and Vivaan were treading along through the rows of people, distributing flowers to throw during certain intervals of the wedding. Hot cuppas of chai and snacks were being circulated, they were more in demand than those Mocha Cappucinos at Tim Hortons right after the first snow-fall. The combination of the light pinks and subtle yellows of the flowers, the greenery of the trees, the blue hues from the sky, made it more picturesque than a postcard from Europe.

Have you ever watched a Gianne Versace show back in the 90s? Weddings were quite like it. First, the refreshers, the very first designs to hook your interest so they sort of introduce the theme of the show, so those were like the cocktail parties, to get into the "Mood" of the wedding. Then came the bolder designs, if its geometrics – the prints get bigger, if a certain hue is being explored – then the shades get bolder as the show progresses. Similarly, as the wedding progresses, the theme becomes less of a mystery and you get acquainted more and more with the bride and the groom. Then, the very last designs are like the shockers but also the "finishers" of what Gianni was trying to portray. He was iconic for his "bandage dresses" and "baby doll dresses" that made a woman feel ageless and forever frozen in time. Much like your own wedding, your truest feelings are intentions for a fruitful future are explored and your loved ones get to revel in your delirium. The wedding was behind her, and she was all set to begin her new life.

CHAPTER 13

"Bhabhi, aaj jhadu-pocha honge?" Leone (their house-help) called out to her as she was done unwrapping the last lot of her wedding gifts. There was like a long, endless row of unwrapped gifts, from the living room, down the hallway, upto her bed-room. All stacked beside each other, in different shapes and sizes, it felt like she was in Legoland, as much excited because she got to decorate her new home in an entire new way.

"Leone, jhadu-pocha shaam ko honge, tum bhaiya Ka lunch banao. Chicken ka masala tayyar karo, dal-chawal ko jaldi tiffin carrier ke andar rakho, garamm rahega." She replied. As Leone began to head towards the kitchen, Tanya called out to her again. "Masala tayyar hone ke baad, ek badhai ko bulaao, paintings and decoration pieces lagane hain." The apartment was one big blank canvas actually and she felt this surge of enterprise and zeal, she wanted to give her home an identity. A painting, when done right in its bourn, speaks volumes without spoiling the imagery or its technique. The abstract and the literal message behind it exist in harmony with each other. Such is the balance (the ying and yang) that Tanya wanted to achieve in her home. No strong, in-your-face messages, but really very subtle hints about the two people that resided in it.

The literal sense of owning a home meant that you made an investment, that you had an asset to your name, but the imagery part meant that you had to give it some character. It had to provide a sense of security, be an introduction to your values and beliefs, your fidelity and pledge to nourish it, refurbish it and protect it against any harm, as it did for you. Your pledge for your home is so reverent because its a substantial argument for your sense of responsibility. Unlike your human kids, your sacred assets, your home won't ever argue with you, but only endures what you had planned for them, be it to their benefit or otherwise.

The badhai rang the doorbell, and spoke up in chaste Punjabi, " ki karvana hain, parjayiji?" Tanya felt like she was back on the premises of Brampton Gurdwara in Canada, this kid was smiling wider than the priest and ready to serve her up some good work in substitute of langar plus a bag of Doritos. Pehle, ye batao ki kis hisaab sey charge karoge? Per painting, per room?" She had to lay it out straight. To which he replied, "Kya parjayiji, ghara Ki bata paraga?" Leone also budded in, "Bhabhi, ye sab apne society ke hi hain, inke saath hisaab kitaab mein thoda dhilai chalta hay! Hum kisiko bahaar se aane nahi dete. Ab Jo hay yehi sab hain!" Ok first lesson in managing your home as a grown woman, you have to have a good support-cadre. Why so? It's because you aren't back in college where you had only two priorities – partying and exams. Precisely in that order. You also had no money and all the time in the world so might as well have done the chores yourself. Being married and working was an entire different scenario altogether. You would be out all the time, but your home needed to be tended to also. Thus, come in the cadre. Leone, "the main gyal", was the Indian version of a proper housekeeper. Then came the sub-cadre, the carpenter, the technician, the ironing lady, the newspaper guy, the gardener and the neighbourhood-aunty. The people in the sub-cadre were pretty self-explanatory, the neighborhood-aunty was like her partner in crime. She was to be "cherished" cause in Tanya's or Rohan's absence, the neighborhood-aunty had to take charge. So, when the hierarchy was established, the emergency crew had to be listed. What was the emergency crew composed of? Doctors – all kinds of them! For headaches, backaches, fractures, colds and the "oops I think we might be pregnant" doctor, she became quite popular on their phone-lists. Tanya and Rohan ran to her at least five times before they decided to get serious about starting a family. Those were some really perplexing times. These were really grown-up times for Tanya. Her mom and dad, all the way in Canada, had given her stern instructions – don't hop onto a flight and come knocking on our door, manage everything on your own.

Thus, she was 100% more alert, 100% more hyper-organized and as OCD as the pricing department at Target. Although like Target, when you invested in your home, be it in form of upgrades or even daily upkeep like chores, you got great value for your efforts in the long-term. Monetarily it made you richer because upgrades make your home more expensive, doing chores made you much, much more resilient than you could ever think of.

Although Rohan helped her out quite a bit, her hours and workload were a bit lax than his, as in she less seized by impromptu conferences and consistent travelling.

Like today, it was a quaint Friday and although Tanya really wanted to check out this club called Social in the Delhi's most happening party-zone called Hauz-Khas, she knew that there would be no solid plans made until like 10 minutes before 10pm, Rohan would make like a phone-call on his way home, Tanya would change and be ready down in the parking-lot so that they could minimize on the time and maximize on the fun. Really the thought of another impromptu (if it all happened) Friday made her feel too distracted from lining her bronzed-vases (set of 3) on this buffet table in her dining area, focusing on alignment and harmony in the house. She then took out this hefty dinner-set, a must-have feature in your house, it was a sign of affluence and style, and began to put them in this antique bookcase that she stole from Rohan's garage full of junk furniture. She replaced the wooden doors with glass ones and widened the gap between the shelves and installed a mirror at the back of the shelves to give it a more glossy look. It was painted in mahogany and matched perfectly with her mahogany dining table. Speaking of this refurbished piece of furniture, when she put in all the crockery and lit the chandelier right in front of it, she felt a certain sense of pride in the fact that she had formulated this house exactly the way she wanted it. Being in-charge of the home, most of the times, she realized her life was really italisized with everything that had to do with it. It was such a self-fulfilling prophecy of sorts, because it demanded so much of your attention, like a feverish child that didn't want to sleep or eat their medicine. Constantly, tugging at your most collapsing muscle, your most irked nerve and your most sharp sense. But, unlike that stiff as fudge child, you had to give into its needs because a home provided you the most emotional security ever. The same security that you probably feel after being married for like 25 years, most couples will vouch for it.

Even though, there were times when Tanya had just finished tidying up the living room, making bill payments online or organizing her winter-wear, when she lay her head onto her warm pillow and permeated into her consoling comforter, she felt a great sense of accomplishment. Also, the same chores that tired her out, made her more responsible for the home. Like, if there was a flickering light-bulb or a malfunctioning of an appliance that was the complication of the day, she couldn't sleep at all. That very same pillow and comforter felt more out of tune in her Zen than ever and she had to take care of them before she went to bed, just like tending to the relentless feverish child.

"Bhabhiji, ab shaam hone ko aayee, kaam khatam karo, kuch khaalo." Leone beckoned her from the kitchen. Tanya was surviving on her third cuppa. "Haan Leone, bas thode boxes bakee hain, ek baar mein saara kaam ho jaayega. Kal sirf saaf-safai. Dinner ki kya tayyari hay?" Nothing took precedence over meals, but it was also always lingering on her mind as a task to get out of the way. "Sabzee kaat di hay, Fried Rice bana doon aur tofu bhi la ke rakhi hay to mix-veg bana doon?"

"Very good Leone, tum pehle-se soch ke rakhtee ho to mujhe bahut khushi hoti hay. Mera 70% kaam kam ho jata hay. Aaj shaam ko tum chuttee lo, kal bahut safai hay, dinner ka mein dekh loongi." Tanya said reassuringly. Tanya got up quickly and followed her to the kitchen to see what she could rustle-up in like 30. She got to chopping the tofu when Rohan called up. "Hey, what are you upto?" He sounded a bit tired. "Setting up the gifts in the house. What time will you be home?" She replied kind of hap-hazardly, fully knowing that he sounded like he was held-up at work. "I won't be home before 10.30 or so. We'll go out tomorrow." There was a long, grasping pause. Rohan began to get worried. Another lively (She truly felt she was the Lively to his Reynolds) Friday to be spent alone. "You there?" He risked it. "What can I do? Its work!" He pushed it. "Where are you going with this? Its like the worst dump-your-wife on a Friday night line ever." She was quite agitated. "Call up Tahira and family. They are always upto something on Fridays." He was in danger zone. "It's great that you have a plan B for me in place, but please make-up for this. We didn't really have to go out but wanted you to see the house, all decorated and stuff. Anyway, get back to work." She let it out. "Bye. Sorry." He let it out too. He was wise enough to cut off the conversation at this pivotal point.

Rohan and Tanya loved coming home in the evenings. Before they got married, they always had to inquest for places to meet. That meant waste of time and money on an open place where they couldn't focus on their lives but just eat, eat and eat more. Their home was like a great hub, sort of a connecting place, where they could let-off their inhibitions and have real conversations. A home, at the beginning of your marriage, can be a great facilitator in amalgamating your spaces together. You define each other's boundaries and then there are times where loves take over and space ends up being just a word in those spellbinding books. They could fight in their pajamas, critique each other's formal clothes before leaving for a party or miss each other awfully when alone.

It was 8.30 and Tanya was parched on her creamed and fluffy lounge-chair, she had placed it right in front of this big window that gave way to a sensational view of the meeting of the vibrant Delhi with the subdued Noida. The vast differences between the two places really dissipated and it did feel like you were watching a painting in motion. The hues of violet, yellows and orange, all being brought to life by the splendor of the moon. The moon, being in the background, was much more in worth and significance to the world, but chose to give life to the sullen trees, the rickety waves, unsettled birds all under the chaperoning sky, ready for an illuminating performance. The entrancing movements of these elements coupled with a glass of Baco Noir wine, made it a semi-alluring night.

She was putting together her albums from their visit to Canada, yes it was still the time when palpable memories needed to exist because gadgets that functioned on our demand weren't valued as much. Speaking of views, she came across their pictures from the bountiful Niagara Falls, there was one picture of her standing in front of it. So excited to be back, each time she flew out of Toronto, it always felt like she was disconnecting out of her comfort-zone, a city that had given her so much. An identity to begin with, and also the prospect of having a permanent home. The next 4-5 pictures were of her on this boat ride right in front of it. Rohan wasn't as amused but more excited to see Tanya's face glistening from the amends of the falls. He was electrified to see her almost dance to the tunes of the surge. This is what Toronto did to her.

The falls, envisaged from the Niagara river, were gorgeous in sight, but being in their presence taught you so much more about immortality. The falls, cascading out with so much vigor, made you realize the importance of permanent objects in your life. For Canada, the falls were a thing of pride and truly a wonderment, because each time you visited the place, it gave you the same feeling of security and confidence. Frozen in the winters, spritely in the summers, and optimistic for the seasons in between. Such was the feeling you got when you were in your home. Permanance, was what it gave you, it anchored your life in a way where you could always sail out towards the unexplored territories and come back to its safe harbor.

CHAPTER 14

If you were to draw a Venn diagram of what a perfect-woman would be, the middle circle would be occupied by Claire Huxtable from the The Cosby Show. For all women that grew up in the 90s, she embodied the women that had it together. You'd never spot her with frizzy hair, outdated clothes, undone eyebrows or battered shoes. Be it in any circumstance.

Her USP was that she was the superwoman without any super-powers. She was the first regular woman with regular dilemmas such as finding marijuana in her son's textbook or working late when her kids had homework or trying to put her husband on a healthy diet. Life, in general is really incalculable because uncertainty leaves room for mishaps. So, when realistic women, grumpy women, confused women and overworked women make it seem okay to tackle problems with much panache and patience, you tend to follow their examples and achieve the same level of perfection. Women, by nature, are generally quite competitive but love to feed-off of each other's insecurities because there isn't a bigger high than relating to someone. You, instantly, stop being too hard on your own decisions.

When Tanya was first starting off her journey in the work-life bewilderment, she had her standards set really high. Because, being good at one thing is swell like the 'chocolate coins' (world's contribution to candies in the 80s) but being good at everything Tanya did was like winning the lotto. Also, being a child of the 80s, she had to be true to the decade that helped shape her values.

Her first ever memory of being made aware of the "tres bien" factor of the decade was when her mother would put on the song, "Aap Jaisa Koi" sung by the singing sensation Nazia Hassan from Pakistan, of all countries. Tanya would jig about to no end, the song was about a woman falling in love with someone and like what would it make sense to a two year old from a nursery rhyme? In the song, she clearly states that she wanted to be with him. Her mom was sort of introducing her to the beginning of a cultural revolution where women began to feel responsible for themselves, if they wanted something or someone, they had to ask for it, convey it and bargain for it with their skills. Till date, Tanya would put it on when she was having a blah time, making her realize that she had to make herself so strong that she could bargain and demand the kind of life, husband, kids and things she wanted. Nothing was impossible if she worked for it.

Was she living upto the standards she had set for herself? She wondered as she was listening to that very song, this time a reprised version by Penn Masala, as she sat in front of her Connaught Place office, with some costing analysis to do, and in no mood to do so. Her mind was overworked,

and gravely craving some coffee. It didn't help that when she looked out of her large windows and saw chaos. It was like 1.30 in the afternoon, and the entire area, reputed by the world's 9th most expensive office market, seemed to be worse than a fish market. It was Delhi in its most disturbed form. Long lines of traffic jams that could never-ever be disciplined by just two-three guards. Vendors permeating into these traffic jams and causing further delays and then just the swarm of people walking in and out of markets, computing more money and also more grime into this self-summating place. This kind of chaos can do a number on your mind, like, if the world outside is so turbulant, what's gonna happen to individual businesses, the little building blocks that contribute to this money-spinning machine of sorts.

Non-stringent work policies, lax deadlines and a lack of hierarchy sure had lead to major delays and confusion in Tanya's work. She was really stressed out because there were times when she didn't know where to turn to, the stress was adding up in a big way. It didn't all happen in one day, one month or one year for that matter. She just left her chair and went out to the balcony and tried to recall where all of this chaos actually began. It was all but the Reagan and his focus on the supply side policies that led to major tax-cuts and infused a great amount of money into businesses.

What did that mean anyway? For most of the world that was still recuperating from the wars, the Great Depression and inflation. More money and deregulation, the highlights of the way economies decided to function in 80s, had surely led to heightened curiosities in consumer spending, but it had also led to a "laissez faire" attitude in workers. Tanya, along with many of her colleagues, felt very frustrated with the fact that they didn't know when they would go home everyday. Month-ends were equally atrocious. They weren't atrocious because of the lax attitude of workers continued, but that suddenly everyone would be expected to tighten up their belts and belch out these amazing numbers. Nandini, one of her colleagues was 6 months pregnant and was burning up in the heat so bad, that she actually flashed us, fully unaware, 5 times in 8 hours to cool off. Tanya was okay with the sight of it but for the guys, it was like having a sloppy, vile burger from the subway station instead of a savoury and plush burger served at the five-star hotels. Saggy, leaky, cracked (the meat) and desperate to be noticed. When you realize that your work, which you are really keen on excelling, is giving you so much stress that you are neglecting your home and family, you won't ever feel about it the same. The only exciting part about working was pay-day. Was it just a phase? How could it be? The same endless cycle of a slow start and then cramming last-minute was too superfluous. When could she ever take control of this situation, because with stress came about disturbed sleep-cycles and hardly ever liking anything about the fun things in life – the same friends that had welcomed her so warmly, didn't seem to get her that excited about partying. She remembered attending a wedding of one of Rohan's very good friend, Ranjeeta Rohatgi at hotel Ashok in Delhi. Now, Delhiites party like its their birthday everyday. It was a lavish wedding to say the least, with the very elite being present there. It was like Diwali, all over again. Every girl dreams of the moon and the stars for her wedding, Riana actually made it happen. What a fantastic effort by the family, it was truly a sight for all of Delhi to see. Tanya, truly felt like she was recognized in this maddening-world of expectations, but only for that night. Then it was back to feeling blah, until she hoped for a promotion. She remembered calling up her dad, and he said, that she had to take the lemons that life handed her and make lemonade. How? "Just stick to it. There isn't a better way to pledge your commitment towards someone by being consistent. Give it back to them every month, your best numbers, your best analysis with your best smile. They want you to cry, but if you smile, you are in a way telling them that you're up for whatever they throw at you. Then, by magic, they will promote you." Great advice from Pappouli, but really, quitting seemed so much more sweet than getting back on the grind. So, work-front was like really 3/5 stars on the success scale.

She was taxying it back from CP back to her home when Rohan called up from Kolkata. He was travelling with his senior. She hadn't seen him in two weeks, she hadn't worked-out in two weeks and she was eating out of take-away containers for two weeks. All because of work. "You're going home?" He asked. "Yeah. Finally, I thought today would never end." 'Ok. Call up Tahira, it's Aadya's (Tahira's daughter) birthday tomorrow. I have left some money on the coffee-table, buy her a gift and call them up for directions." He continued. "Tomorrow! I can't do tomorrow!" She put her foot down. "You should go. I won't be back until Wednesday." He firmly said. She wanted to go, Tahira was the very first gal-pal in Delhi. Besides her awesome sense of humour and bodacious dancing, she would take off at any party, she was great with her advice. She was married to a busy-lawyer like Tanya, and she was like two years ahead of her in every way, be it managing her home, raising her kid or dealing with everyday concerns. But Tanya felt like crap, everything that she wanted, was slipping out of her hands. You always learn something great from some great women along the journey of your life. She knew Tahira would be very excited for her first-born's birthday so she wanted to be a part of it. She also knew that she would throw a great party, be dressed like a million-bucks and make sure everyone had a great time, as much as she was. That positivity was so infectious, that as soon as Tanya stepped into her house, she ran to charge her phone and got the details for the party.

She got the details and then plopped herself on the couch. One look around the house and she was about a tad-bit away from feeling "grody to the max" again. It was calling out to her. The way you take care of your house isn't the same way you someone else takes care of it. Even when her mom would visit, Tanya would always supervise, while her mom micro-managed. "Bhabhi, khana kha lo. Mein sone ja rahee hoon." Leone beckoned from the kitchen. "Leone mera khana microwave mein he rehne do, mein kuch kha ke ayee hoon. Is hafte ka hisaab do mujhe." Like she would even be able to concentrate. Leone showed up with the paper and pen, that smelt more pungent than the vegetable market does when they get their first-lot, early in the mornings. She turned on the radio to the vintage-80s station and the song, and Pat Benatar comes along, so apt for the minute. She began to sing along, loudly, "That's okay, let's see how you do it, Put up your dukes, let's get down to it." She put her feet and Leone served her a hot cuppa. "Phir se coffee, bhabhi kuch kha bhi liya karo. Pet mein baccha kaise banega?" She tried to care. "Leone jake so jao. Tumhari advice mere bas ki nahi hay." Really, the things happening in her life were hardly digestable by her system, much less having a kid. She gulped down her coffee and checked everything on the list as they logically matched upto their respective prices. Trying really hard to achieve a balance, while intoxicated on caffeine, fighting it out with might rather than only hope. Your body is your temple, so you need to look after it. But, what really gets your mojo back into form is mainly your favourite food, great conversations and good music. It was that time of the night when she listened to her favourite songs until Rohan came home. This hadn't happened in a while. She was so angry. Angry at the fact that her world seemed to be spinning on a different vertex. Her temper seemed to flare at the littlest things, the more she took on her plate, the more she became unsatisfied with her life. So to kind of pull the plugs on it spinning out of clout, she spent like an hour unwinding the hands of time, sort of savouring the last hours of the day to get a grip on things. But, there's good sense in this emotion. Some of the best music comes from this very emotion. Like a "with or without you" from U2 that highlighted the pangs of waiting on the acceptance by your beloved or a "the one I love" by R.E.M that makes fun of us becoming too fixated on things that give us both frustration and pleasure, be it momentarily. It was music for the soul with the most heart-wrenching lyrics. We, as humans, began to feel really protesty in the 70s but became loud and angry in the 80s because the protests fell onto deaf ears. Be it protesting against nucleur wars, government incompetence or blatant racism, music (fame) for artists became a "right to passage" to convey their inner angst against the calamities of the world. By becoming "cheerleaders for peace" in the world, they sought to sell their souls for the betterment of others. If the artists were doing it on the world scale, so were normal people with extended hours of work and minimum wages. Music was a great way to heal from the erosions caused by human actions. Soulfool, or rather soulful music no longer made sense. It was more straight-up like a "hit me with your best shot" or a "let's get physical" or a "call me". The anger sure made us take action, like Tanya began to clear-out the newspapers from under the coffee-table that had piled-up, the half-empty food containers stuffed in the fridge or the unchanged bed-sheets from last week. She was so tired, that didn't even think she'd wake up on time the next morning for work.

She was again taxying it back to work the next morning, looking like a mannequin from the stores lined across Las Vegas wedding-chapels. Wearing a frail white frock, glossed-out with make-up and eyes looking like right after her hair had been burnt from her hair-dryer. What else could she do, but to shock herself out of bed, for another grind? She began to put on maroon nailpolish, on a moving cab, she was so sleepy that it looked like a much milder colour than it actually turned out to be, so she ended up looking like a big vanilla ice cream with toppings of red cherries from her loud make-up.

She remembered that before getting married, she had a "look" for every season, that adhered to the sensibilities of a workplace, but she was overworked that she didn't realize that she was trying too hard. There was no time to create "looks". Upon entering her office, she began her initial "hellos" and realized that there wasn't a person that seemed comfortable with what they were wearing. Sitting awkwardly in their very padded chairs, tugging at their shirts and letting out big sighs as they noticed their clothes completely wrinkly from the back. They were all one fashion disaster after another, waiting to happen. In between generating these "eat my shorts" ratios, she began to search for clothes to wear for the big birthday party. She went to the "Vogue" website. It was smack in the middle of summer so it was mostly about resort-wear, meaning, bathing suits mildly covered-up in fabrics you'd call maxis or sarongs. Really, Delhi wasn't that far behind in bold clothing than Paris, Milan or Tokyo for that matter. Delhi women were almost about an embroidered or a mirror-work gladiator away from the rest of the world with regards to being fashionable. At par and at ease with their bodies. She felt so irked by these swimsuit models because she hadn't eaten properly or worked-out in a long time. Everytime you feel "dry" about yourself, you turn to comfort clothing from your childhood days to balance out your rummaging hormones.

Tanya had decided, she was going to wear, she managed a smile as she realized that all models weren't emulatable. From her decade if she could swear by one style that continued to "psych" the daylights out of everyone was the black dress with the big-cut in the front. Cindy Crawford, back in 1989, had given the dress an almost icon status. The monotone fabric, draped so exquisitely that it just melted the most imperious egos in men and boosted the most vulnerable spirits in women. It is also the only garment that can never change its perception of the "mender of many relationships" irrespective of its style, cut or drapery. On the one side there was Benetton that splashed out and explored many colours, showcasing models from all races, but on the other side, couture designers, explored the very same colour in its variant styles. Where is Benetton today? But, the black dress seems unfazed in its qualities. Black is simplicity and versatility personified in those very flawless ratios. Precisely the way men like their women.

She was about to mail-out her numbers, that were going to be mended several times, because you don't really close until the midnight before the first day of the month, so she wasn't as nervous as she was about wearing her dress after binging like a whale. You really can't mend faulty first-impressions of you after showing up in crappy clothes amongst people that belonged to Rohan's work-circle. Her phone rang and it was Lisa. She was Rohan's college-friend's wife. "Hey Tanya, kya kar rahi hay?" She sounded quite delighted, so unlike Tanya. "Hey Lisa, about to leave work. Whats up?" "What time are you going for Aadya's birthday? Want us to pick you up?" She knew she was miffed that Rohan wasn't going with her. "Theek hay, what time?" She tried to sound appeased. "Hum 7.30 tak aayenge. See you then." She hung-up. Tanya was thankful for this cherished friend circle that Rohan had established, they seemed like very formal because they were supposed to be professionals. But, they partied like those "bad to the bone" frat-boys that aced their exams with as much vigor.

The party was great, the ambience was awesome and the cake wasn't to be missed. They were driving back and Lisa and Nick were fighting like two screwballs because Nick drank too much and Lisa's only mission in life was to curb it. All she could hear was, "Bahut ho gaya, bahut ho gaya!" It wasn't amusing anymore, but you had to give it to her for being so relentless. Such is "L'amour vrai" (True love). She requested Nick to turn on the retros-80s station.

It was a bizarre night of sorts, Tanya was looking out the window. There wasn't a star in sight, no pleasure of the carefree winds or the tangibility of the clouds that chisled in the light of the moon. Everything seemed so stiffed and burked in the brink of summer. No respite from the soaring temperatures. With her folded hands and head kneeling on the window, her gaze was still on the opaque sky. Lusterless without its embellishments, the stars, and impenetrable by the ferocious moonlight. Even when stripped off of its augmentations, it remained unfazed by the nasty gazes of people that didn't seem as interested. Aap Jaisa Koi came on, perfect timing to conclude the night. She adjusted her spandex, boon from the 80s, and put on her white shawl as she opened the windows further. What an amazing feeling to conclude this chronological phenomenon of a decade in every which way. Path-breaking ideologies, rebellion music, defected beliefs and renowned sense of identity for women that needed as much of recognition in the world as the men. Tanya's confidence was on like a 70:30 in ratios and she wanted it that way. There always had to be room for improvement, else she wouldn't get out of bed the next day. Imperfect ratios yield the most fervent desires. If there weren't any desires, there wouldn't be so much optimism, delirium and promise in the line, "kaash mujhpar aisa dil aapka bhi aaye". Its the 30 in the 70:30. The 30 that makes you giggle every minute and the 30 that makes you want to be agile, the 30 that helps you process the 70.

CHAPTER 15

When something extraordinary happens to you, you begin to have extraordinary expectations from yourself. It is unfair to you because you put yourself on overdrive, as the ability of your body and mind to create these very miracles should be sufficient enough to make you humble about this gift in your life.

Why would it be sufficient? Tanya would realize only after she had given birth in the midst of this ruckus because she had spent her entire pregnancy phase trying to be the "mommy-of-everyones-dreams". Rohan and Tanya had spent most of her pregnancy apart.

Here's the saga from the beginning:

Tanya and Rohan were seated at "China Cottage", a regular venue for their friday-night dates, sipping on vodka-cranberries for starters. They hadn't been out in a very long time. Rohan was busy building this office, which he had bought just like a month before but they had been conceptualizing it for a long time. He was quite excited, he had built one room specifically for Tanya in it so she could carry out her work from there or that she could hang around while he was held up. It was also to double-up as a conference room but he actually thought it to be where his future-family, meaning kids et al, would hang-out while he worked. Mind you, neither of them liked to be disturbed while they worked and liked working for hours together without many breaks.

"I think the office is coming along great. I've been too busy for us, but we need to get away for a break. Where do you want to go?" He asked, nicely. She was the reason this office even existed.

Their home was getting too crammed with his files, collegues and clients. Tanya had suggested that he shift-out so that he could only focus on work and then focus on home when he was home. They didn't realize but they had begun to plan a family in the back of their minds already.

"I think we should explore a bit more of the weekend-getaway resorts in Gurgaon. But can we get a booking sooner?" She replied. "Well, it was going to be a surprise. But Poppy Resorts (15 km out of Delhi) a client of mine has lent us their deluxe room, with an adjoining spa, we can leave this Friday and be back Sunday night. "Awesome! I have a week to wind up at work." she was stoked. "It's been quite hectic trying to keep this office at pace with work piling up and running in and out of courts. Thank you so much for understanding. We deserve this break." He squeezed her hands.

The week sped by really fast. Tanya was packing for their trip, but she had been feeling quite bloated, thus she hadn't eaten at all. She had just rushed home from work and started to sort out her clothes. It was only for about 2.5 days that they were going to be there, but, she had packed for five different ocassions. When she checked out their package and the facilities that their resort had offered, she was stunned at the assortment of them. All thanks to media, for glamorizing a simple, getaway.

Delhi, being so metropolitan, hardly had any nature-backed or resource-backed factors to capitalize on weekend-getaways. Unlike Canada, that had many. Tanya was reminded of the many little comfy-nooks in form of cottages and weekend-resorts that were placed along the wineries in various regions of the country. The two most famous ones were along the Niagara-on-the-lake and Prince Edward County. They had the comfort of the suburbs because they were secluded and surrounded by so much natural sunlight and greenery, and most importantly they had this "old-world" charm to them. Moreover, you got to drink some really authentic and delectable concoctions nature can ever offer. It's altogether, a very innocent and unaltered juxtaposition of what love should really be.

She packed two big carry-bags full of clothes for swimming, spa (sauna, jacuzi, massages), ball-room dancing, hiking and general "resortwear". Fully knowing that their lazy-butts would only be plopped on their recliners and rush down only when the food was laid-out. But, in these fast-paced times when people are busy creating these "wannabe identities" via social media, why should the couples be left behind? Couples these days create an identity on social media together because they get to double their liking, spectators and overall presence. So general categories that you got to see on social media are: athletic (marathons, adventure sports) religious (pilgrims, sunday mass) and romantic (writing poems for each other) amongst many. Thus, companies capitalized on this by offering these array of activities to encourage communication and intimacy in couples. A loved-up weekend can do wonders for a couple in monotonous lives.

So, they were driving up-to the resort and they hadn't had anything to eat. In their 4-hour sojourn, he insisted on eating at four joints, all her favourite cuisines, she wasn't feeling it at all. She was bloated to the max and was only surviving on starbucks iced-teas and lattes. She wasn't able to even endure the smell of a slice of bread, much less strong spices. Rohan was worried but thought it was her being moody because she wasn't getting much of his attention. Little did he know, there was going to be much more whining and sobbing coming along his way, and in what magnitude.

They checked into the resort. Their room was a deluxe suite with all the amenities. "Let's take a dip in the pool and cool off a bit. Change quickly. I'm going to block the pool for the next two hours. I'll be back in 15." He ran downstairs to get them some robes. Only when he got back, Tanya was fast asleep on the bed. To his shock, he put her under covers and turned off the lights. He went for a swim instead.

The pattern of sleeping more than usual and hardly eating would continue for the next 2.5 days. He kept coaxing Tanya to eat and be a bit more active. Tanya wasn't too bothered because she thought her body was only trying to recover from the slogging at work. She didn't realize that she was experiencing the very first signs of pregnancy. She quite liked the ball-room dancing, even though she was bloated in her "high-low" dress and a Tamilian version of Toni Braxton, in every way – appearance, accent, big hair, bigger hips, even bigger lips, screaming out the songs in a more shrill voice than kittens when they're first born. She was so tired from her work that she couldn't really gage on the first signs at all. Nonetheless, it was a fun weekend, to say the least. She must have shed like 5 pounds with no food and only ayurvedic, body-toning massages.

"You need to get yourself checked by a doctor. The same one that you keep running to when you think you are pregnant. This time, you might be." Rohan told her while they were driving back. "Are you disappointed that all I did was sleep this weekend?" She asked in a very sombre voice. "No I think this break was necessary for you to try and understand what is happening. You might be pregnant." He said sternly this time. "Your defense mechanism towards anything new or a big change in life is to ignore it or delay it. I had to literally convulse you out of Toronto when we were about to get married. It wasn't that awful. What are you so lax about now?"

"You know me. I need time to grasp it all in. Talk to me. Make me feel like I'm up for it, cuz I really am. I am craving a family, some powdery faces and toothless smiles." She said with a smile.

"Go get youself checked. That's the first step." He said. "What if I am? What's next?" She asked excitedly. "After its confirmed. Which I know you are. Social media will take over. I don't have to do much really." He joked. She was shocked that he was so sure about it.

It was a bizarre Monday because she had forgotten her hair-dryer back at the resort, forgot to set her alarm and left the tea-bag with boiling water on the stove for the longest time. The preggo-brain was kicking in. She didn't know to react. She was on her way to the doctor's office, and took a deep breath and just left everything in God's hands.

There couldn't be a bigger reality check, to ground you at your core, and to also make you realize that your perception of yourself is most important than anyone else's perception of you. You need to be strong and stringent in the way you lead your life, self-actualize your worth in your eyes first. People on social media can see through lies, but they can't see through your struggles. They shouldn't be able to. Your struggles are yours to commit to, to own upto and to shape them in a way that they become your triumphs. Your struggles are to be actualized to become the forecasts of your future, your measure of happiness.

What she saw next, knew no bounds of happiness. A tiny, amoeba like structure, overcast by a cloudy nest of sorts. As she began to focus, she spotted a tiny shell like structure that was quivering at a constant-rhythmic pace of like 3 seconds. That was the heart. A live, beating heart. The noise was like when you're in an empty room, in the winters, with no ventilation of sorts, and your ears begin to hiss from the cold. Exactly like it. Only you're no longer alone anymore. Her hands and feet were colder than the jelly that they put on your belly during the ultrasound.

"Congratulations Tanya. You're already 10 weeks along. Everything looks great. Hearbeats are a strong 90. That's **your** kid." Said her doc.

"Smriti. I am 10 weeks along, meaning?" Tanya was hysterical. "It means, its confirmed. You're pregnant. You need to start with your meds and your diet." Said Dr Smriti, taking charge of the situation.

"This is amazing. When is my due date?" Tanya asked. "We'll know it a bit." She replied. "Will I know if its a boy or a girl? I mean, I don't know how I'd feel with a boy and his boys bits inside me." Typical Tanya, and her racy mind.

"You can opt to find out at 12 weeks. You'll be back in two weeks for your first full ultrasound of the kid."

Tanya was handed an envelope with the title "Baby of Tanya." Her due date was on November 1st. From then on, time stood still and Tanya's mortality was attested.

Rohan was home early, and was hysterical. "You should have come to the ultrasound with me, it was so bizarre. The baby is like only a faint light like thing, it shakes, quite curiously, like those jellyfish that you spot at beaches. In two weeks time, you can see the entire kid, we can count the toes too!"

"I am, for sure, going to be at the appointment. This is great." He couldn't stop smiling. He ran upto the bedroom, opened his closet, and handed her a book by Dr. Spock on pregnancy and nutrition. You should read this and refrain from those monsterous websites that can send you on a complete tailspin." He said.

"Where'd do you hear about Dr. Spoke from?" She asked very quickly. "Ahh, someone sent me this link and I got a little carried away and did my own research on the best books on pregnancy." He replied.

"Research? Where? Like some chamber in court" He was caught. "It was this website, on the net." He began to laugh. "It's a great source of information, it's like your parent minus the scoldings. You get to stay current and informed on alot of the topics." She said.

The next two weeks really went by fast, with Tanya hauling her bloated self back and forth from the office. The good thing about working while pregnant is that you get to be focused on a task. Pregnancy, which Tanya was beginning to realize, was very taxing on your body, and it isn't under your control at all. One minute you are nauseated like you've been living next to a sewage tank and the next minute your hogging three burgers after "fasting". One minute you are sweating because your hormones are raging and the next minute you are burried under a big blanket because your feet are cold. Thus, Tanya had decided to work throughout her pregnancy so that she could compensate for the anxiousness surrounded by this confusing phase. But, that wouldn't last too long either.

One evening, on her way back from work and she was about to fall asleep when her taxi hit a big road bump and she almost flew across to the front of the car." That was a shocker. She got off and ran upto her washroom and noticed that she had spotted a little. She called up her doctor and was asked to come into the hospital right away.

A quick ultrasound later, which were 5 of the most nerve-racking moments ever, everything was okay. Much to her relief. "This was really touch and go, Tanya. Early pregnancy is very tricky, I advice that you take leave and be home. The chord of your placenta is very short, you need to take rest. Take some time off work and be on bed-rest." She was angry.

Point noted. Soon enough, Tanya was on the net, typing away to a state of dippy about this particular pregnancy condition. Low and behold, like 17 websites popped up and after reading about four pregnancy diaries of these celebrity bloggers, she realized that it wasn't something to be ignored. No condition, even as small as a pimple on your nose, could be ignored. It always, snowballed into something else, that's how sensitive her body became. Oh and speaking of sensitivity, the mood swing train can drop a load on your loved ones like a serious bomb on a plane!

She began to fight with Rohan, he couldn't handle it. Every morning, she complained that she wasn't feeling okay. Rohan, from his busy work schedule, barely could take time for her. So, he began to shout back. "Stop cribbing! You're about to become a mother. If you yell at me, I won't be able to help you. I don't want to be around you anymore. As exciting as this can be." He was screaming.

He couldn't help her. He had too much work, that's the way it was and it had been since they got married. Family was a priority, but it only was after work. She was home because she taken a maternity leave until her doctor said it was okay.

"I feel like crap!" She yelled back. "Take care of it. If you scream and cry, which is all you do. You will never delivery a healthy child." He said it, and left. His car sped out faster than ever. He wasn't going to have it, certainly after the kind of demands at work.

Tanya cried for like two hours, and then she called up Nandini, her collegue that truly revelled in her pregnancy. Nandini decided to meet-up with her for lunch.

It was a cool afternoon at Eros Hotel, Nehru Place and Nandini showed up, looking like Posh did when she first delivered during World Cup, undainted and heavenly. There was a perpetual halo around her. Her kid was spotless and giggling like there was no tomorrow.

"You need to be heard. You're feeling lonely because you have no goals in life. Pregnancy can make you directionless." She said. You need a blog. Tanya thought she was going to sermon her and was actually in hopes of some valuable advice. She just simply said, you need spectators. Go on the net, make yourself a profile, shop till you drop, do prenatal yoga and join mommy-support groups. Give yourself an identity, a presence on facebook. You need to start living the life you want to live." She said.

"That's all it takes?" She questioned it. "Yes. Pregnancy happens to 1 in every 8 women in this world in their 30s. That's how common it is, it brings you so close to so many women in the world." She said, forget the fact that its taking over your life, only remember that its made you a person that every women can identify with." She said.

"It doesn't help the fact that these very women comment if you eat a chocolate bar everyday or didn't take prenatal vitamins before planning a pregnancy. I mean, its my child, right? I should be able to make decisions on its behalf and everyone should accept it."

"Tanya, it doesn't get any better. But if you are having fun in this, then it only helps you. It helps your moods and then your overall health. Please, stop worrying and start realizing that it happens only once or twice in your lifetime."

Lunch was done. Tanya was enlightened.

Much to Rohan's annoyment, Tanya took to the net and decided to write her own pregnancy diary under her own name – Tanya's Tummy Tales. He was glad she was off his back at least. They had stopped communicating, that was their way to "cool off". Days went by, it stayed the same. Silent treatment was the way Tanya had laid the rules for effective communication early in their relationship. Baselines, according to her, were: ignoring - she was angry, silent - he had it, cutting his calls - there better be some diamond before any "cuddling" happened next. Those were the various stages of her annoyment in their relationship. Words, ironically, her forte, became less powerful when handling situations with her most loved ones. She ignored everybody she loved when she was annoyed with them. It was like posting an update on social media and the person you expect to like your picture first, never notices it at all. It's less piercing than words, but more prominent in its conveyance of your feelings. When someone's too used to your appreciation, they won't let you be annoyed for a long time. One very important lesson that social media can teach you.

Her posts consisted of weekly updates, complete with the kid's vitals such as – heartbeats and ultrasound pictures. Some posts consisted of interviews with her doc, videos of her doing prenatal yoga and tips from her dietician. She even took out videos of her getting some really exotic messages. She wasn't trying to glamorize her life, like the celebrity mommies are criticized of doing, but she was actually appreciating her body. It wasn't being fake at all.

When Victoria Beckham or Demi Moore pose in leading magazines, it isn't to inflate their egos or to intimidate you, but to encourage you to raise your standards of good health and good living. You can never take motherhood for granted, but cherish it.

It was a big high! It was a great way to connect to the rest of the world, with real women in her "perceived reality". There isn't a more normal feeling than being able to relate to a women in Botswana that has the same cracked heels as you and a woman in Sweeden that has a sinus infection like you during pregnancy. Their perceptions only come secondary, they are formed by you and you only. You are in control of your own perception, first. Thus, it is your perceived reality, your realm, your conditions and your contentment. You can never carried away with 1000 more likes or a 1000 more smilies appreciating your efforts, you learn to react positively towards situations. Maturity isn't in fighting it out with your might, its in being silent and tactful. And doing it with some amazing clothes on.

Before she knew it, she was out and about, enhancing her life and health, only to make herself better so she could be a better mother. From creams that take care of dry skin to almond milk that helps you remember, to stylish clothes that enhanced your curves, she made it happen for herself.

She learnt to become more responsible, she began to shop wiser, depend on good deals and be aware of the realities that await you when the grass isn't so green, the burnt part of the pregnancy-pie. Basically, its your consciousness to change with situations, regardless of what medium of support you adopt, that matters. You have to self-actualize, you have to gain insight of what's happening and you have to tread along, never stop.

Tanya was in her 35th week of pregnancy, and her and Rohan were about to leave for a Diwali cards-party. "Tanya, hurry up! I don't have 5 hours to spare. I need to prepare for a hearing tomorrow." He called out to her.

She stepped out in a black saree, yet again, with a halter blouse. Yup, you better believe it, she was rocking that too and some emerald earrings. A tinge of red lipstick and some golden slippers completed the look.

"Which celebrity have you copied now?" He was being such a pooper. He loved her in black sarees. He was the least bit interested. She was losing him. He began to shut her down, his only concern was the child.

The party was fun, Tanya got everyone's attention for the way she was glowing, the fact that she looked like she was really having a good time. People were guessing on the sex of the baby, its birth-date, its birth-weight and its names!" She noticed Rohan's gaze on her, but it was more of a concerned look, because they weren't speaking to each other anymore. She had been taking care of herself all along, doing it all alone while he was busy working.

He came upto her and whispered to her, "I'm so proud of the way you've handled yourself. I've hardly been around. You look fantastic. Tiramisu on the way back from Eros Hotel, I promise."

"Awww!!" Is all she could say. Perception, created. Ability to change, rewarded.

It was a magical night, it seemed like all of this time in waiting for their child had gone by in a whiff, but actually, Rohan was holding his breath all this while, just pushing her away was his way of dealing with stress of a pregnancy. He just buried himself in his work. Barely even making eye-contact with her. The most anticipated moment for parents-to-be is the birth of the child, and it seemed like it was smooth sailing.

They got home and Rohan got a call from an angry client. "What do you mean? It's never in our hands! We never get to sway things our way...."

He was back to yelling, the doors were jittery from the coarseness in his voice. Tanya began to panic. She ran towards him, he signalled her to go into the room.

Ten minutes later, she heard the plate flung across the room and hit the floor. He had asked Leone to serve him some of the vegetable pie she had baked for her pregnancy support-group. It was nothing but a mess on the floor.

"Damn it, why don't you deliver. This is too much stress for me. I can't handle it anymore. Please go in the room." He said.

"Calm down! You're scaring me!" She tried to scream.

He walked out of the house, once again. She tried to run after him, breathing heavily. "Bhabhi, don't run." She grabbed her hands.

Tanya was crying. She sat down and two hours later began to feel some piercing pains.

"Hello, Dr Smriti here"

"This is Tanya, I think I'm in labor."

"Come to the hospital. Right away."

She was being wheeled into the OT, her body numbed by labor pains and her mind numbed in shock from Rohan's screams.

Fifteen minutes later, she broke-out from shunning of each of the two into bouts of laughter when she heard the most loud and awakening cry.

"Congratulations, Tanya. It's a girl. Almost 5 pounds."

"Can I see her?" Tanya asked.

"We're taking her to the NICU."

She was wailing, marking her presence. Etching her own identity. She got that from her daddy.

O God, anything but that dreaded four-letter word. Tanya was bombarded with visuals of all these parents rushing in and out as various surgeries were done on their newborns, crying their lungs out.

She couldn't let herself break-down, now. All this time, she learnt to be brave. Her perception of herself was that she could change the situation in her life with just some courage and composure. She couldn't let herself down. Her child was dependant on her.

She was too tired, from hours of labor that wasn't progressing naturally, because she was in a state of panic. Letting herself down in her own eyes. So much for perceptions. If this situation had happened ten years earlier, she would have been in a bigger risk at life than her child. Time and resilience had brought her to this juncture in her life.

Perceptions stem from an aspiration to create an ideal self, you usually take tips from various people and sources, so it isn't necessarily yours. Identity gives you that authenticity. You're very own perception of you, as per you. Perception is you on the outside, really. The way you present yourself to the world. Identity is innate. It's etched in your being, it's literally manipulated by your DNA. You can change your perceptions. You can't really change your identity at its core.

For Tanya, perception wasn't really in Rohan's anger, Nandini's words of encouragement or Smriti's words or caution, it was the inferences that she chose to make. For Tanya, her identity was based on her consciousness to change, to make herself more resilient.

And thus, Selena's shrill cries, a true reality, were brought about in this very balance of trying to educate herself and purposely making a big facade of it. If you don't bring attention to it, the world will forget you exist. She was going to be the mommy-of-her -dreams, and everyone better appreciate it.

CHAPTER 16

((And where is this little birdie going?"Tanya chimed in as she maneuvered her right arm with a fork wielding a piece of french-toast toward's Selena's mouth.

"No mo." She tried to convey it while waving her little wrinkly, hand at Tanya's face. It was a total, "talk to the hand" in a very pleasant way, though.

Selena, all of two years old, was propped up on this glass-top patio table in their balcony on a nippy winter morning. Solids and her weren't really "besties" yet. She would have preferred her comfy formula-milk and bottle anytime, but was slowly treading her way into this phase, making her opinions known. Specially to Tanya, her mother.

"Birdie go to Kan-nn-a-duh" She said with a big grin as she created bubbles from her mouth, Tanya broke into giggles. She knew how to make her mother happy. That was the magic word. It was her trick to get her mother to sway towards her wishes. Great communication skills. Precisely what Tanya wanted.

"Okay time for a bath." Tanya picked her up from the table and put her in her crib. She was preparing her bath with warm water and ran to her cupboard to get her clothes. Selena was too big for her crib, and was flagging her mom to come and get her because she loved bath-time. She never stood still or was too engaged in things that would distance her from her mother. Tanya was her only contact-point, rather the axis upon which her world revolved, the only person that understood her to the Tee.

During bath-time, Tanya sang songs to her, in Hindi and English, and Tanya followed each of her actions. Amidst so much activity around her, the washing-machine just behind them in the balcony spinning in full speed, the kitchen abuzz with noises of the utensils and appliances and the television expelling nursery rhymes also, she was only focusing on Tanya's eyes. Droopy and hysterical from the endless feeding-and-changing cycle, they loved to watch Selena create different and unique memories everyday. Today, she was this thriving, curious and commanding child, all because Tanya hadn't lost hope. Two years back, this same child was a helpless, frail and delicate bundle of emotions that didn't realize the significance of its own existence.

The very first night when Tanya had garnered enough strength to take care of her own child, Selena was brought into her hospital room as per her instructions. The wooden cot, sustained by wheels at the bottom, was drawn in. It had white bedding, and this little fragile bundle, squirmish at just a touch, was trying to get acquainted to the world, with its own cautious pace.

If she was a kid of a relative, Tanya would have rushed and picked her up. But, a mom's instinct suddenly kicks in, faster than drugs kick into your senses. She backed off, sat beside her on the couch, and watched her sleep peacefully. Rohan would come late at nights after finishing work, today he would be in for an awesome surprise.

Selena would hopefully be up by then. She wheeled the cot close to her as her couch was nicely placed by the ginormous, floor-to-ceiling windows that gave way to the view of Central Delhi. It was an almost frozen winter night, frozen by Delhi standards. Meaning misty windows, foggy streets and sporadic rains. All contributing to the "hawkish", wintery factor. The radiating street-lanterns under the coral-hued sky was captivating, no matter where you were in this world. Five years ago, she was in Toronto, under the same luminating sky, downing martinis and devouring a big-fat rosti in the midst of a winterfest of sorts. Its was termed as Winterlicious. These winter-fests, mostly to highlight the season combined with Christmas, consisted of live concerts, night markets with vendors from around the country and restaurants belching out various delicacies to tap into the festive spirits. Back then, it was all about exploring the city, making the most of the season, shopping till the last dime and meeting as many new people as possible. She really had no care for anybody else, only her little brother that waited on her to bring booze and leftovers for him because he had limited pocket-money. She wasn't too bothered about her parents also. No responsibilities meant pure bliss, but it also meant that you were putting off a life that fulfilled your desires to have the kind of money, assets, kids and spouse that you wanted. Because Tanya paid taxes, volunteered for charities and always was up for another night-out with friends, didn't really mean that she was leading a wholesome life. She was just in plain denial about her age.

The one thing that never waits for you, is your age. The sooner someone communicates that to you, the better it is. With age, knowledge and responsibilities, you learn to react with less emotions and contingency.

At present, it was all about her daughter. She had become nucleus of her world. On this solitary, winter night, her ears were abuzz with the chaos around her birth. It had been quite a testing time for the two as parents. Rohan only got to see her at night, so it was Tanya that took charge of Selena's well being.

During her visits to the NICU, she realized that parents were communicating with their tiny tots. Moms were singing lullabies, dads were making faces. These kids are tiny, frail and panicky. Their bodies have to undergo one test after another and endure surgeries to survive. Their only cheerful moment is when their parents, the only ones that care for them, engage them into a world of songs and lively conversations so that they can hope for a life of good health and elation.

The first-time that she walked upto Selena's crib, she didn't know how to react. She had spoken to her mom, and her mom had told her to only focus on her child.

"Hey Tanya...what's the update today?" Alka tried to sound cheery as she held back tears.

"5 pounds...stable... vitals are ok...accepting feeds well..." Tanya's only reply on when asked about her health.

"That's good. I wish I could tell you to take care of yourself. But please, until she is out of the unit, please only focus on her. We are on the next flight. Love you." Alka disconnected the phone.

So the task at hand, for Tanya, was to make her daughter realize that her fragility was only temporary and that she could come out a champion. Selena was her responsibility, she had to react responsibly. Her life was no longer hers, it belonged to her daughter.

Responsibilities teach you accountability also. They contribute towards your character development. That you have to be answerable for them and the more they thrive, the more strength and resilience you gain from it. But the linear (upward) and steady growth only happens if you react responsibly also. Five years ago, Tanya would have been hysterical, she wouldn't have 70% of the courage or tact that she had today. That only comes with age and experience. Its like watching a 5 year old have a tantrum for a toy and a 15 year old bargaining for it by doing chores around the house.

"Its time to feed her."   A nurse called out to her from the nursing station.

"Is she on 2 ounces still?" Tanya asked her as she watched the nurse prepare her feed.

"Yes. Please feed her slowly." The nurse instructed her.

Tanya was handed a bottle with her formula and she eagerly went to feed her.

What's it with moms and trying to overfeed their kids? Tanya was more eager, tilting her bottle more eagerly as she drank, wanting her to finish.

She then realized that the tot had a mind of her own. Yes, this tiny speck had a mind of her own. She would begin to spill her milk from the sides of her mouth, and began to shake her head. She was communicating to her, that she was full. After this, Tanya realized that she couldn't have her way with the pint-sized kid of hers. Being responsible also meant that she had to accommodate for her feelings also.

Unlike unhuman responsibilities, like your job or your assets, kids have feelings too. You have to handle kids with more patience and understanding. You have to realize that you can only get them to be on the same plane as you if you hear them out.

You have to step back, you just can't be overbearing or aggressive. If you truly care for someone, you can't push them to a corner and make them do things your way by virtue of guilt and oppression. It's good for your sanity also.

When Selena felt comfortable by Tanya's presence, it was only after she realized that she was being heard. Her cries were ignored by the nurses. But if she had to be taken out of the unit, from under the close watch of the nurses, Tanya had to gain her confidence.

"Okay kiddo. Look at me. Do you want to sleep?" She said as she picked up Selena from her crib under the garb of many clunky monitors.

She was a bit whiny, very sleepy and her frazzled eyes looked up at hers, she was pleading to be let out of the unit. Tanya began to rock her back and forth. She began to cry. Tanya's heart melted and she realized that her daughter was shaken and very weary of the things happening around her. She got up and began to walk and swaddle her to sleep.

"I find your lack of faith disturbing." She said to Selena, the dialogue said by Darth Vader in Star Wars.

"Sleep. You want to sleep. You need to sleep. We'll play tomorrow. I'll get you out of here." She told her as Selena began to close her eyes. Soon, she was asleep.

"Never tell me the odds." She slapped on another dialogue from Star Wars as she put her back in her crib. Selena was no longer dependant on the nurses, she had endured enough from them. She had a new bower for her survival. It was Tanya, her mother.

"I love you. I will never let you down." Tanya walked away from her.

Communication is a two-way street. More needs to be said and conveyed because if things aren't communicated properly, then that leaves lots of room for inferences.

That night when Selena triumphed and was brought back into the hospital room, Rohan and Tanya watched her sleep. They could be excited about being parents, after that big hiccup of sorts.

"I told you, that you and her were going to be okay." He told her as he held her hand.

"Have you recovered from the state of panic?" She told him as she managed to finally be smiling.

"What do you mean recovered?" He retorted. Now, he could be angry at her. "If YOU hadn't panicked and cried after for hours together, you wouldn't have labored!" Tanya couldn't believe what he had just said.

"What should I have done? You left in such an angry state." She retorted.

"You were the one that was pregnant. You should have acted wisely." He stood up and spoke up.

"And walking out on your pregnant wife is what on barometer for wiseness?" She was angry.

They both heard Selena wake up. Rohan ran and he grabbed her. Then, they shut up. End of conversations. The onset of many hazardous inferences.

Many arguments later (they never screamed or fought) leading to her or Rohan running to rescue Selena, that responded to arguments in bouts of cries and shivers, they stopped communicating.

The breakdown, a culmination of pressures from around their fishbowl existence, was so severe that they only spoke about their daughter. The foundation on which people build their marriage, was shattered.

Tanya was losing out on him, all in the midst of struggling to give Selena a healthy and wholesome existence. They hardly spoke, they were sinking into this suffocating ocean, that engulfed them each time they chose to swim out of the hefty waves of expectations.

It was nothing but a bunch of unrealistic expectations that they bestowed upon each other. The last nail in the coffin was their fifth wedding anniversary.

Selena was tucked away in her crib for the night. She slept so peacefully that Tanya began to cry. Their existence together as a couple or as a family had begun to seem fake. Like it was all made up, day in and day out, they were living in monotony, but disrespecting each other's feelings on many levels.

Rohan came into the room, trying to post a smile on his face, giving it another attempt to spruce things up in the romance area. Tanya was reading a book, facing her back towards him, ready to sleep. He knew, that if she was reading right before sleeping, with the kid nicely tucked in, the house gleaming in cleanliness, then she was in a good mood. He crawled into bed beside her and gave her arm a gentle nudge.

"So, have you taken the home pregnancy test?" He asked.

"Yes I did. I thought you'd never ask!" She turned and got up to sit right beside him.

"And...?" He knew that smile on her face.

"The home pregnancy test is positive. I took like three of them." She said. "But then I have booked an ultrasound on Thursday to confirm things. This time, I hope its a boy. Reyansh. Your choice of name."

"On that note, I also have a surprise for you too." He said.

"What is it?" She asked.

"I am throwing an anniversary party for us, at Light House. You can't drink though. I don't think you'll be too sad about it either." He said.

"No vacations. No drinking. No late nights. No high heels...." She began to laugh. Their absolute last attempt to create some sanctity in their marriage. To complete their family. To move ahead in life.

Actions speak louder than words. This gesture was sweet, seemed too good to be true.

Reality was too hit her with a big blow...

It was the night before their anniversary party Tanya had picked up her outfit from Vero Moda, a purple blouse with a short skirt. He liked it that she showed off her legs, it was also her staple garment.

Her phone rang. It was a missed call. She then checked her whatsapp, to get an update from her mom's playgroup on a playdate for the next day.

She came across this video sent by a random person with a message.

The message was along the lines of a random lawyer, guaranteeing her a sizeable portion of Rohan's assets and saved-up money if she believed the video he had sent her. The video had questionable content in it.

It was 2.5 minutes of the most disconcerting and dejecting visual ever. The two people in the video were kissing each other...at some party...

Tanya deleted the video. But she couldn't erase the memory from her mind.

She was numbed at their anniversary party. All of his work-circle friends were there, Rohan had given Tanya strict instructions to never act lude or dance seductively with him in front of them. Usually they were really cool and great dancers, but today she was stoic. The lights around her were spinning faster than her head ever had. People came to greet her and they just seemed like those scary, floating mannequins on train rides at amusement parks during halloween. They might as well have been speaking in Vulcan. The room seemed bleaker and bleaker, it kept fading away as the night crept in. The day seemed so flawed, the celebration seemed impaired of love, the good-life had prematurely ended. The vicious cycle of trying to resurrect a marred marriage had sped past her...once again

She had become peeved at the chronicity of ongoing and repetitive conflicts in their life...an absolute red-flag in a marriage where two people no longer communicated...

CHAPTER 17

Spring had sprung after three long, dolorous months of winter. The first flickers of the sun bathed the room in its entirety with much sanguiness. Tanya was back to working at the same school that Selena was enrolled in. She was trying to create a spreadsheet of the parents that had enrolled their kids for the spring-summer activitites and to keep a chronological record of payments made by them. While focusing on work was only secondary, Selena was the first thing and the last thing on her mind. She never missed an oppurtunity to walk by her playroom and peak into her windows. The one big happy moment in her day was to see her daughter thriving, learning and participating.

Tanya had spent the last five months pondering on where to proceed from an important juncture in her life.

It took one very important phone conversation, with Rohan. Timing is everything. It never waits for you. If you don't convey what you want to, if you don't ask what you want, then your words become nothing but sapless news.

It was after her book-launch of her very first novel. In the midst of all the stress and chaos that led upto her separating from Rohan, he clearly had told all his friends and well-wishers that they were separated, she had managed to yield out an earnest representation of where she felt today's society stood with regards to their beliefs on marriage.

It wasn't only ironic, because her's was falling apart, but it was also the reason why the separation happened. The society, that mainly helps in lineation of our beliefs, had changed with regards to marriage, co-habitation and relationships.

Are we ever interested in yesterday's news? It isn't significant because its lost its value in time. It isn't worthy of anyone's notice. Indeed its a buildup or a genesis towards a parable, but it isn't sensational because it isn't current anymore. People have changed their opinions once today's news is published.

Thus, if we are so accustomed to changing our opinions on meaningful matters (headlines) on a daily basis, we can certainly break-down age-old opinions on marriage and what is acceptable in society.

The book-launch event was an eye-opener. Tanya had come across quite a few of these instances in the past few months or so.

Many people had attented. Some of them were Rohan's friends also. Tanya had prepared a speech, there was also a speech by her publisher. Oh the ways in which they argued and yet trusted each other to bring out their best work ever. By the way, the relationship of a publisher and an author is very much like a marriage. The publisher is always looped on curbing creativity and making books more attuned to popular culture, basically, the narrative should make money. They have managed to tap into what people want to read today, thus, its all about what is good today.

She was dressed in a chiffon blue saree with black flowers. With her signature pearls and she stuck by her mantra for life - to show up feeling and looking like kohinoor diamonds.

Selena, dressed in a black party dress and silver shoes, was creating a ruckus with her squeals and tugging at her mother for attention. She loved the spotlight too.

"Great turn-out. You seemed very confident." Said Harjeevan, Tanya's publisher.

"Thanks, Jeevs. You helped me bring out the best in me. " She replied back as she shook his hand.

"Today's pictures will be sent to Delhi Times as a press release piece. Your pictures, as always, have turned out marvelous. Let's hope your words reach out to as many people as they can." He told her as they shook hands.

In the midst of their conversation, Alka tapped her from the back.

"Tanya, I'd like you to meet Lilly Aunty and Ashwin uncle." She said.

"Hello. Thank you so much for coming. I really appreciate it." Tanya said.

"Do you remember Bhawna in Toronto? Tanu's friend from London?" Alka nudged her, as in please refresh your memory. Every mother has that "nudge" or "look".

"Oh yes. They had just moved to Toronto. I remember." Tanya actually remembered.

"Yeah. They're her aunt and uncle. They have come here specially for your book launch. We go way back, like almost 30 years, we've spent some great childhood moments in Patna. Now they're in Delhi, itself." She said.

"We are very eager to read your book. Your speech was very good." They said in unison.

"Thank you." Is all she could say.

Tanya was basking in the ambience. She was moving ahead. The book was like her outlet to be connected to the world. To reach out to people rather than getting bogged down by the waning presence of Rohan in her life.

Thankful that so many people, from Delhi, her adopted family of sorts, had shown up to support her. They were as eager to read her book as she was to share it with them. They strenghtened her belief in humanity, and that being current with the times was the way to success. You have to make an attempt to make it on today's news, nobody lives in the past.

Then to be reminded of Toronto with family being present there, Bhawna of all people. She reminded of her cousin, Tanu, because they all loved clothes. Clothes, just like, your thoughts, your writing, help you express yourself to the world. Outdated clothes, like outdated thoughts never made sense to anyone. Bhawna and her would visit these outlet malls, that had the best brands and were great equilizers in terms of quality and pricing. It was a way for a country, so rich in history and diverse in cultures, to bring such a large population on the same plane of trends and unity. There was Bhawna on one side, and then there was her brother, Neil, that completely defeated the purpose of such mechanisms. He made so much fun of us for trying to be thrifty. For a brown kid (slang for Indians) he seemed really averse to such "phenomenons"as Tanya would like to call it. For her love of clothes, style and trends, is what had evoked her way with the words. She could swear that the leather jacket he was rocking, could might as well have been bought at Alfies in London. The way you look really enhaces the way you feel. So she didn't find it funny, and then on top of that - he kept "frontin" about this big-shot of doctor he wanted to be. He kept naming all of these exams that he wanted to take, and it was like Persian for Tanya. But then again, what she remembered was that, he made his sister laugh with all of his jokes. British accent + dry sense of humor, never go out of trend. Their perennial, surely.

Speaking of living in the present times, Tanya was extracted back with Selena tugging at her. She had, had enough of her mother gamboling around in the spotlight. She was longing for her.

Except, Tanya had to make one important phonecall, in order to begin the closure of a marriage that had begun to lose its significance in her life.

Was Rohan okay? With Selena in her arms, she grabbed her phone and ran outside to call him.

"Hello?" His coarse voice made her teary-eyed.

"Hey" She said.

"Are you in town?" She asked.

"No. I am in Chandigarh...   I have to go. I can't talk." He said.

"Rohan...wait..." She was eager to speak to him. Selena was whimpering, wanting to be cuddled to sleep.

"Why is she crying?" He could hear her.

"Uh...I...uh...today has been very special....I feel...are you listening?" She was stammering.

"Take care of her. I have to get back to work. She sounds sleepy." He hung up.

Outdated, incomplete conversations. The trend continued. Three months had passed by since she had moved in with her mother.

The entire world was moving ahead, at lightening pace, but Rohan continued to shun her out with his standard replies.

"Damn it, Rohan. Either finish it off, or think of a new line." She said loudly. She walked back, it was cold and Selena needed to sleep.

That conversation, albeit being very mundane, had rung alarm bells for her. This was a very significant day in her life, and neither her nor Rohan cared to be included in this momentous ocassion. This meant that they had made peace with each other in a way, that they were moving ahead in their respective lives. It was indeed a loss in a big way. Losing a life-partner meant steering your life on your own and actually doubling your responsibilities. Deciding to take each day at a time, make most of each day, tread a little faster, a little longer, work a little harder everday, the goal was to be current everyday.

The party continued. Harjeevan and her edited out the pictures to be published the next day. She was also filling out a questionnaire from a magazine while Selena lay asleep in her lap. Fighting back tears.

CHAPTER 18

It was going to be a super-busy day in school for Selena because she was going for a picnic at Lodhi gardens. She wasn't coming back until later in the evening, so, Tanya decided to work in school until she came back.

She was doing an analysis for a big meeting the next day with the head of the school, so she was able to be focused on work also. It was good to be back at work. According to Tanya, to work was always the best reaction to "crisis-management" in one's life. Provided you had your other responsibilities in check. Your mind was focused on the task at hand, your body was also coping up with being busy all day and it effected your overall health because you weren't stagnating. It also gave you alot of positivity, and you were compensated for accomplishing some great feats. Anything that builds up your resume is worth savoring. It's an investment in yourself.

Her phone rang.

"Tanya, we're in the front of the school, come to get her." Said Noreen, her teacher.

"Ok, I'll be right there." She saved her work, closed her system and ran, more like sprinted, to greet her daughter after her excursion.

"Sunshineeeee" She screamed as she ran towards her.

"Momma, look, flawah" She had gotten her a rose from the garden.

"How was your day?" She tried to sound chirpy as she picked her up .

"Did you have fun?" She asked as she picked her up in her arms.

"Eat smilies...then drink juice..." She tried to describe her picnic.

"Wow...okay" Tanya replied

"Play with ball...there were white birds" She wanted to tell all.

At home, in the evenings, was homework time. Since Tanya was working full-time and Selena was in day-boarding (after school hours), they're only together time was homework and park.

Today's homework was to write a story on her picnic. Tanya helped her write it and it turned out quite like this:

We went to Lodhi Gardens today. It was a bright, sunny day. I played with Priya and Kian. We drank Frooti and ate smilies. There was a duck and we named it Bob. There was a cat and we named it Dora. There was a bird and we named it Gian. We played with ball and watched the Wind-Mill spinning. Maam taught us many songs. It was fun to do so many things together. We laughed alot.

(This will be printed in aanya's handwriting).

These were purely Selena's thoughts. She was great with her descriptions. She described all the living things with reference to their emotions and non-living things with reference to their characteristics. She had learned to appreciate the valuable qualities in everything. By this, Tanya was happy that she had learned to give meaning to things she came across, her words became her tools to get acquainted with the world.

Words, when incorporated into your understanding of the world, can become a mechanism for your thoughts that lead to a fulfilled life. They have the power to help, heal and share your thoughts.

But, on an individual level it can be like a self-fulfilling prophecy, where you can align your words with your thoughts, and then your thoughts with your actions. It gives you the power to assert yourself towards progress, growth and prominence. Thus, there is a direct corelation between words and outcomes.

It can garner you many feats through vehicles of oppurtunities also. Her boss at school, Jassica, had read her book and was quite impressed.

The next morning when Tanya buckled-up for the crucial meeting after dropping Selena off, Jassica called her to her office.

"Hey Tanya, come in." She greeted her and pointed towards the chair.

"Hey, good morning." She walked in, rushed with her "deliverables" in crispy, white printed documents.

"The forecasted numbers from last season were quite to the Tee, but it being spring meant that we could expect the actual turnout to be accurate with the projections, for the fall and winters, we need to be a bit more realistic in our baseline numbers." Jassica pointed it out to her.

"By the way, before we begin, I want to congratulate you on your book." She said quite cheerfully.

"Oh! Thank you. I'm glad you liked it." Tanya replied. They proceeded with their meeting.

"Tanya, hang-on, for a minute." Jassica called-out to her.

"Yes?"

"Would you like to develop content for us? Like, you're great with numbers, but, I can hire anybody to do that. While you're with us, why don't you write for us too."

It was a great offer. Tanya couldn't say no.

"Okay, what do we do?" She asked eagerly.

"Tomorrow." She replied. Tanya left the room.

The next day, Jassica began to explain to her that she would create content for all of their posters, adverts and kiosks for their summer activities. They had to plan ahead and the content had to be expressive and fetchy.

For an avid writer, that only focused on shaking-up the values and beliefs of her own generation, she had to think of content for like 5-10 year olds. Also, her target-group wasn't going to be people that were going to learn from it, but, they were going to invest time and money on it. It required much more thought and attentiveness.

To be paid for a hobby, more like a passion, is like the icing on the much devoured red-velvet cupcake, but it was also a great confidence-booster.

Her readers were "sampled" out, and, thus, she had to provide value for money. But you couldn't really delve into your fantasies and cause an intervention of sorts by fictionalizing people and legitimizing their believes. You had to be straight-up and to the point. Which can really curb your creativity, then writing really becomes a job.

She got busy with fostering content for the school's activities. Summer really brought about some radiant efficiency in her.

She was charged up to see the kind of response her words would garner.

Could she ever think of a career in writing? It would be sacrilege in her father's eyes. He wasn't very keen on her taking it up as a career. He straight-up told her, "don't waste my money if you want to become a writer! I will give you my basement instead (for free) and you can begin writing from there". To which she laughed. Thus, the number-cruncher in her was born.

Today, he was unwell, plagued with memory-loss and very much becoming the needy child that she had once been to him as a perplexed 12th-grader that didn't know what to study. So much more of him was rooted in her than just their common love of numbers.

It was almost June and the school was reverberating with posters and kiosks of her writing. Only empowered women can build up other women. Speaking of which, she was to get another big oppurtunity with regards to her writing.

Her aunt called her up from London and she had a relative in Delhi, a very famous and accomplished television-personality also with a flare with words, and she wanted to hire a copy-writer. It was a big favor and it would really catapult her writing to the national level as it was a national-level news channel.

Her name was Anita and she called Tanya up one busy afternoon as she was in the midst of interacting with parents after school. Tanya was so comfy in this little school, with her kid right next-door and a very understanding boss. She wasn't speaking to Rohan so she didn't want to turn to him for help with Selena. The hours were so flexible, that she would be home by 5pm and only focus on the kid. So she decided to give it a miss altogether.

"Hello" Tanya's voice was very rushed.

"Is this Tanya?" She asked.

"Yes. Hello, Maam. Good to hear from you." She managed a reply, although she was shocked that she called her, herself.

"Tum kyo nahi ayee, interview ke liye." She asked, very politely.

"Haan, Mami ney mention kiya tha. When can I come?" She had to ask, screw being the comfy zone. Her mom had said that she would help her out.

"You can come next Wednesday at 11.30 am. Just speak to my secretary, Ranjan, and confirm the appointment."

"Thank you so much, Maam. I'll call him up."

She went home and spoke to her mom about it, seriously. Her mom had enough on her plate with her son studying and an ailing husband. Yet, she said that she would help out with Selena because such oppurtunities came around once in a lifetime only.

Rohan's parents had also offered to help upon hearing of such an oppurtunity, thus, she knew she could manage.

So, on that very destined Wednesday, she headed to Anita's office. Excited and clutching onto her write-ups. They were two news articles that she had written - one being on Vijay Mallya and his trials and the other being on Manish Malhotra launching a new Pret line.

The taxi dropped her off at Station 24, she was amazed at the vastness and expansiveness of the space. Really seemed like its originator's dreams had been realized into reality, and it was being nurtured so.

She met up with Ranjan, and he led her into Anita's office.

"Hello maam, hope you aren't too busy." She managed to speak a sentence.

"Aao. Bhabhi (Tanya's aunt) batayi humko tumhare baare mein. Ek position hay yahan, copywriter ka." She proceeded.

"Ok. Thanks, Any oppurtunity, in this platform, is one of a lifetime. Thank you so much Maam."

"You're welcome. Join from June 1st." She said with a smile.

She was very down-to-earth and yet very confident in her position. She truly felt like she deserved that place and that she had earned it. She truly owned it.

Why that date? It was a good two-weeks away. Tanya was ready to dive into this place like you are ready to dive into the pool after a super-Siberian winter. Great stretch for the body and a great tuning for the mind.

From Selena's expressive descriptions to her own ability to put thoughts to paper...she continued to be mesmerized by the inventiveness of words.

Your words, very much, permeate from your subconscious mind. Your unconscious memory is said to be perfect. It is a store, of sorts, for all your life events that have happened. It is also responsible for your responses, since it operates purely from memory and previously learned behavior.

If you are committed to positivity and always moving towards betterment of your life and uplifting the life of others, then you programme your subconscious mind with tools that keep you consistently aligned towards your motives and goals.

There are times in life where you feel unmotivated and that you are stuck in a rut of continuous behavioral patterns and befogging emotions. In order to change these patterns, you need an "affirmer" of sorts, to tell you which way to lead your mind and then the mind, once received these signals, will get working towards it by alloting all of its resources on it.

Your affirmer can be a person or the bible, they only become your guardian angels of sorts if you learn to trust them and that they will uplift your life towards success. The affirmer is more significant than your soulmate and they are more in love with you than you will ever know. They are so committed to you that consciously you respect them and subconsciously you live in their reverence.

Tanya's affirmer was 6,693km away and she didn't realize it then. The pattern towards a changed life and a renowned sense of hope was being systemized and she was learning to breathe, let go and let him steer...

It wasn't his intellect but his strategy to create this belief in her that she could pull through from little bouts of self-doubt and regain her confidence, again.

The first step was to join at Station 24 on June 1st. She did exactly that.

CHAPTER 19

I t was a very peculiar morning, her first day at Channel 24. When things are supposed to fall into place, they really are.

Tanya was dropping Selena off to school. She had been speaking to her about starting at this new place. She wasn't going to be in the same premises as her anymore. Thus, it was a true "detaching of the umbilical cord" moment for mom and daughter.

On their way to school was when they had their most consequential conversations. She was somewhat able to convey the change in their daily schedule to her, but just in case she hadn't been able to grasp it, Tanya reconfirmed.

"Monkey, mamma isn't going to be in the same school as you anymore. You are okay with it?" She asked her very keenly.

"No lunch time?" She asked.

"No. You have lunch with Tina okay." Tanya was hoping it was okay.

"Okay." She said as she clutched onto Tanya's hand.

"Do you have momma's scarf in your bag?" Tanya was going somewhere with this.

"Uh-huh" She seemed unfazed.

"After lunch, when you wash your hands, you can wipe your face with it."

"Okay. It got your perfume?" That one detail that she was disquisitive about.

"Yes. Lots of it. Momma put three sprays."

"The Pager Perfume?" She meant Pleasures from Estee Lauder.

'"Yeah that one."

"We'll do homework in the evening. You can call momma from your tab also." She patted her back, assured that she was going to be okay.

From having her daughter latched-onto her for days together when she was an infant to being in school full time was a journey of sorts. It isn't your fault though. Their size and their fragility, when they're born, actually get to you. You begin to concentre them in your life with every other priority orbiting aroud them. Their lack of temperance is and their despair towards the world is a big provocation towards your confidence level. It's purely because you love them. The love is so unconditional, because their yours, that you will overcome all obstacles to get them acquainted with the world. You want them to succeed, you want to gain their trust and forge that bond of trust. It only stems from love. You dote on their milestones and guide them religiously, making them independent and building a secure attachment.That's why our parents become irreplacable in our eyes.

She walked into the office and was greeted by her new boss at the reception. His name was Rohit Seth.

"Hello Tanya, welcome to our team." He tried to be pleasant.

"Thank you. Very excited to be working here." She replied.

You will be a part of the department that is responsible for creating content for our two websites - Station 24, the English website and Namaste 24, the Hindi website. We are a team of 8 people. I am the head and the rest of you will be working under my guidance.

"This is your seat, turn on your PC and your collegues will teach you how to login to our websites." He said.

"Okay, thanks." She said as she sat down at her work-station.

Basically there were two ways that you could post content onto these websites. One was via newswires, large (updated) databases of news stories, the other was conceptualizing your own stories.

Tanya was asked to post 20 stories everyday from the newswires and do a write-up also. She was given a fixed number of stories and the topic to write on and it could be of her own choice.

Albeit it was a new job and that the stories she published onto the website would be read by everone in the country, she didn't feel any pressure or like she was being tested. Within the 9 working hours daily, this task was more than accomplishable. Specially in a country that is ctiticized for really creating slaves out of their employees and compensating them with nothing much more than basic salaries.

The other employees, her collegues, could post an unlimited number of stories and they had to write many more stories everyday.

Could this be because she had just started working? Her family was very much aware of her marital status, and they were worried that she might be under some stress or might even breakdown at some point. She was experiencing some sort of withdrawls because she would have little bouts of crying every now and then.

Divorce proceedings had begun, Rohan's family had initiated it. They wanted to proceed with divorce in form of a settlement.

Tanya's family wanted to fight it out in court. It meant a prolonged decision with much mudslinging happening in court. So then, she was back into the same fishbowl sort of an existence. It's one thing to be married into a well-known and well-connected family, but its another thing to try to please everyone and then end up in a rut and get all stressed out and unfocused again. This meant that she kept tugging onto Rohan for his assurance and becoming less confident in herself and more insecure in their relationship. The time that she was married to Rohan, she didn't get a chance to take a few steps back and create a balanced and realistic plan and create a secure attachment towards him. She just kept moving ahead with life and handling with whatever came her way with an unfocused perspective.

But, the best solution to this was that to follow one person's plan of action, their methodology, and then live peacefully. This doesn't breed any insecurity or bouts of anxities or periods of crying because that person's plan of action is right. More importantly, it adheres to everyone that is a well-wisher. It helped her create the work-life balance that she needed. The USP of it was the pace of the workload, it was steady and it wasn't overbearing. Thus, she was able to build back her confidence, bit by bit.

London, in contingency with life, was like an intoxicating carnival on wheels. While cars nudged passed those mighty red buses impatiently along the roads, minicoopers meshing in and out of traffic, men in suits making money from their glowing offices halfway into the sky and the palaces were forever weaving tales of fantasy playing out in reality. The romance and authenticity of Shakesperean standards combined with a dope night-life.

By some chance beneficience of the destiny-making Gods, he happened to steer my interest and heighten my intrigue for him when I got to know about him, as in him becoming a part of my life.

Rich, educated, attractive, funny...What was I getting myself into? It only took me like a second to redress my doubts, because he was cute.

He meant alot to alot of people in his life. They were so attached to him. Be it besties from university or subordinates at work, they seemed to be at ease in his company. Exactly what happens when you're at peace with yourself. He seemed like the most surreal, disorienting and downright dreamlike thing that ever happened to her. Tanya was in love with him. She wasn't sure if she was shocked because she knew this moment would happen or if she wanted him to quiesce or fight for her. She was in awe of him.

The one factor that truly made this reverie a reality was when Selena brought about his name in one of their conversations. They were speaking, connecting, bonding...she was fond of him.

Neil Verma, didn't just suffice but surpassed expectations of what a secure man was to be. The best part was...he never shut her down, no matter how unsure she was of herself.

Thus she felt secure in this vision of the pegged life she wanted for herself...

"Do you think Rustom will beat out Dangal's record this award season?" She asked her collegue, Asha, while posting a piece on it.

" I don't know about the awards season. But it will make the money. At least 200 crores." She replied.

"200 crores seems so achievable these days."

"Yeah. But only wholesome/family entertainers make that kind of money. It isn't the deal with all kinds of films." She added.

"So it's worth posting?" Tanya asked.

"Yes. Definitely." She confirmed.

News stories, irrespective of their genres, were always clinging onto the bearings of this rating system created by websites based on the number of reads they got. Money wasn't surely the motive behind it, but also they were

competing for likeable content. Or so it seemed. But, these newswires were so attuned to the needs of the readers that they had managed to build a confident and set reader-base. They had become popular because they were reliable.

The motive behind any sort of authority-subordinate relationship is being reliable. You can communicate that in only so many ways. Repetition is a killer and being confident is the key.

Right after dinner on a school-night, Tanya was putting Selena to sleep. Usually, she would carry Selena to bed after a bath in the summers. But lately she noticed that Selena would want her to read to her instead. No lullabies, no bathing and no little-kid stuff. She wanted Tanya to be in bed with her and read these short stories that instilled a good habit in her and also made Selena confident in her ways of comforting her. Putting a kid to sleep is a tough job, and, you can't really faulter at it. It's tought to get your child to be independent without feeling comfortable in your parenting. After reading for about 30 minutes each night, she would get comfy and fall asleep on her own.

Your reliability will come off as a confidence-boost in them. It forges a relationship of trust and permanence between the authority and the subordinate. They begin to respect you once they see that its for their benefit.

There is also no better joy in reciprocating that confidence that they have in you by obeying them. By listening to them, reasoning out their concerns for you and achieving your goals under their guidance. Secure attachments are formed when they exude warmth, realistic expectations and are emotionally tuned to your needs. Your authority has to have your best interest in mind. It's their consistency versus impatience, its their calmness versus irritability and their fondness versus demands.

After a while, you yearn for them, you want to make them happy. You want to strenghten that bond that they have laid the foundation for. Your success isn't just yours anymore, its their benevolence on you. Their ardent halo on you...

CHAPTER 20

From a world of number-crunching to purely pouring out your opinions with contours of words, work seemed more like play. The industry was different but work ethics, standards, quality and competency requirements remain the same. After a certain training-period, you are left to swim up the ocean of expectations, slowly maneuvering your skills.

She remembered, almost a decade ago, when she was studying for gmat exams, and she scored a solid 650. She had 2.5 years of work experience and her recommendation letters from her previous bosses praised her tons on her working abilities. It was a beginning of her career in finance, and she was superbly stoked about it. She had really put in alot of hardwork and had endured much criticism by her bosses for being too racked about her own work. She had learnt to be self-reliant because her work was solely her responsibilty.

However, being responsble doesn't mean you had to keep working on a task for ages and ages and never garner any success on it. It won't only be a hindrance towards your growth, but also will make you very averse towards your work. That's when Tanya learnt the wonder of having a Plan B.

Her initial days at work at Station 24 were pretty breezy, albeit the media industry worked non-stop to supply the most current and accurate news to its consumers. Posting was really doable, and creating your own narratives were actually a no-brainer if you had a knack for words. But, there were alot of times when she was conflicted between setting new benchmarks, as in thinking of innovative topics to write, or only posting away the most current news to glory. It was because she had learnt to always have new expectations from herself at work.

The first year was pretty smooth sailing, with her doing exactly she was asked to do. So, the work-plan decided for her was totally apt for her. Between divorce proceedings and child custody concerns, it was really tough for her to focus on work and be very productive.

"Tanya, come out for lunch with me. I want to try Thai food at the restaurant next-door." Asha, her collegue, called out to her. She often sensed Tanya tearing up.

"Okay. What about everyone else?" Tanya looked around at all the other collegues that were busy on their PC's.

"No we are okay. We will eat later." They all said in unison. Great friends, even better collegues.

Seated at the restaurant, Asha and her spoke about their daughters, her daughter and Selena were the same age.

"It must be very tough for you to be going through this situation with a small child." She was truly concerned.

"It's tough. I guess its cuz you've seen be breakdown quite a few times." She managed a reply.

"Yes. I am also a mother so I really feel sad for you."

"Thank goodness for this job. Else I wouldn't be able to get out of this stressful marriage."

"Life always brings out the best is us in some way or the other. Kuch na kuch raasta nikal hi aata hay." She said.

"Yes. Plan B always exists. We need to have the courage to follow it." She said.

"Thanks Asha for all your help. You and everyone in Convergence."

"You're welcome. You can talk to me about anything. We are all always there to help you."

"It's enough that you console me and you all try to feed me every now and then." Tanya didn't forget to mention it.

Why were alternatives in life called Plan B? There is a somewhat negative connotation to these two words, when put together. On a sidenote: it's also actually the name of a world-renowned pill to prevent pregnancy. Again, it's like the absolute last resort if you don't want to be pregnant, but also the most effective when taken within 72 hours of intercourse.

Thus, the focus should be on its strength, success and the fact that it's still within the scope of your happiness.

It doesn't have to be out of the norm, nor does it have to have a seal of approval from everyone around you. It only means that it is the best choice for you and your future.

People, generally, change their career-paths like thrice in their lifetimes, but as they do, they become more resilient and strong.

Doctors are known to be placid people with an impossible job. Irrespective of where they work, the scenario seems to always be the same. There are too many patients, too few doctors and nurses, and too few hours in a day. Was he ever satisfied? Did he ever feel like the captain of a sinking ship? Was he like running around vainly trying to close the loops caused by voracious ailments. Did he feel validated, while on his rounds, because he had worked really hard for his extraordinary grades and praisewothy recommendations? Had he mastered the skill of explaining what takotsubo cardiomyopathy was in less than a minute?

He seemed to be smiling in all his photos on facebook. She often looked at them in disbelief. When you are in a field for more than 12 years, your work becomes second nature to you. Tanya was sure that he knew all the relevant surgery procedures by heart. Also, that he would be surprisingly knowledgeable about each patient, and crisp and efficient in his diagnoses. He must be indulgent, concise, frightened, brave, gentle, competent and considerate all at once. All of this was expected of him and he was able to do it because of his dedication. Truly, worshipping his work. Most of all, she thought he would be nicknamed Dr 007 - licenced to kill cuz he wasn't too diddly on the eyes either.

That's some consistency and love for what you do. It certainly wasn't for the money. But then only when you love what you do, you go so far.

When working in finance, be it in Canada or India, she felt as if she was being pulled in all directions because during month-ends, you needed to align the functions and numbers of all departments to get your final numbers.

But, in media, you're only working in one section, so you're focus is only on that one "job" that you have. As much as Tanya loved the high that she got from delivering great work, like two hours before midnight on the last day of every month, she could really breathe easier in this field.

She felt really balanced, like the balance she tried to achieve when she had first moved to Delhi.

She was back in control of her life, she was able to spend quality time with her daughter and she was able to squeeze an hour of workouts every now and then at the gym right next-door from her office. It made her feel more at peace with herself than ever before. She truly began to give her best at work, to be able to be productive rather than regressive. To keep-up rather than be old-line. To gain insight on its significance in her life than only live paycheque to paycheque.

Similarly, in life, when Rohan nabbed her out of her comfort zone, she thought it was the best possible option of a life-partner for her, but really, its the person that catches you when you're most perplexed is the most perfect plan, the most perfect option, the most perfect life-partner for you.

How do you know you're going through your Plan B (Plan Best) in life? There is a linear (upward) growth between the alignment of your priorities to your success.

With this though, Tanya was ready to call it a night as she enlisted a cab to pick her up in 10.

"Are you about to leave?" Asha called out to her.

"Yeah, my cab's coming in like 10." She replied.

"Okay. Before you go, just post the pictures of Kareena Kapoor's big birthday bash. All of the Kapoor clan were there and she cut the cake with Saif. She looked amazing in this golden dress."

"Alright. I'm certain I'll get 1000 views for it." Tanya smiled.

"Surely...and change the heading of post to "Bebo's Big Bash"... or a flashy name."

" Thanks Asha. Will do."

CHAPTER 21

((Tanya, don't forget to eat your sandwich before you leave for work." Her mother called out to her, right before she left for work. The same way that she called out to her when Tanya left for work back in Toronto. Years later, she was still the nurturing mother to her, perking her up each morning with her witty sense of humor. She surprised Tanya with the way she was so confident and comfortable with herself.

Nothing is more impressive than a person that is secure in the way God made her. Tanya's mother, Alka, had it all throughout her life. Talented, educated compassionate, understanding and truly an unselfish mother.

Married at the tender age of 21, she had been convoyed into a life of triumphs and sorrows by her husband. She never complained of the sorrows and she always reveled in their victories. To her, the life that she had been given by him, was an invaluable gift. When she began to lose him, the astonishing fact was that she didn't crumble...

It was a tough battle for Tanya and Ayan, watching their father trying to swinder out death. The visual is one she would want to forget, but wouldn't be able to. The person that took his family from the laundering and sublime streets of a small town to one of the most inspiring and industrious cities in the world, boundaries that transcended time, culture, values, beliefs didn't mean a thing.

I low could you strain a person, that truly bargained the best condonations from life with his hardwork and determination, with death? The complete shut-down of the functioning of his body was unfathomable for him, because he had obeyed all the rules, and became a winner in life because he played fair.

You don't really value someone's life until they succumb to death. It's really like a surrendor of sorts, because its an inevitable force. Thus, death doesn't really erase a person completely off of the face of the earth, it reverses our perspective on what is actually bestowed on us when we're given life. From birth to death, we strive and struggle for longevity via means of wealth, name, fame and kids. It's a limited time we're given with unlimited oppurtunities, too bad we don't realize it until our time is up.

For the ailing, Life can also be viewed like an ongoing war and death can be viewed as peace. In order to free yourself from the hardships of life (to attain death), you must combat with them, with all your will, taking every chance given.

Leo Tolstoy presented the two as a virtue and a vice. According to him, war was like a social evil to avoid and peace was like a virtue to be aspired for because it was liked by all. Sidney Sheldon, on the other hand, presented the two as cause and effect. One leading to another, one being responsible for the other. Be it natural calamaties or your own neglect, it is a result of the way life happened to you.

Either way, loss is loss. Nothing compares to living with your loved-one. Tanya's mother lost her sire. He had given her the works - they travelled extensively, she felt protected in his homes, she was educated by him, he showed off her artwork, gushed about her cooking skills and was in awe of the loving mother she was. She had meant more to him than he was to her.They were truly two pieces of a puzzle that enhanced and completed each other. No doubt they had their share of fights, but they always retracted towards each other, the forces of attraction and trust were stronger than the forces of grudges and loathing. She was moving ahead in life, without him, but with all the love and the many gifts he had given her...

You get to see love in all forms today - but the love for family garners you the most gratification. It's also because human bonds give you a sense of belonging, lonliness and sorrow have no place in a home that is occupied by a loving family.

Sometimes, they are people that live outside of your home but very much in your heart, that remind you of it...

They were all walking back from a musical fiesta, past ardorous emporiums and huge, monumental buildings. It was 10 minutes to 2am. Their minds consummated in the enterprise of morphemes, visuals and melodies. Great way to tap out of tedious work, they reckoned. His legs were aching from the dancing, his ears still ringing from the euphony and he must have never felt more gratified than in his long nights at the hospital. What a treat to share with peeps you practically grew up with. Truly, in good times and in bad.

Days later, the same kid was experiencing bouts of euphoria while devouring a football game. The greenery, the exhilarating crowds and the whirlwind of history-making moments that are realized on the pitch. In the days of podcasts and live updates, he still chose to get out of his hectic work-life and watch it live. Hours later, they were soaked in the rains, the raindrops frisked their hair, the drops seeped down to the back of their collars, but they barely felt them, so submerged were they in the delirium. Boys will be boys.

He wasn't selfish with his life, many of us like to tread through our lives with being cornered and isolated, and slowly work towards our goals because we fear criticism. With the bombardment of media into our homes, our private lives are no longer private anymore. So, Tanya, for the sake of her sanity, would work on her growth in confined spaces - be it a corner spot in the office or a corner spot in her home. He loved the crowds, he loved the gush of screams that palpitated in and out of stadiums. Much in appreciation rather than slandering. He was one of the world, sharing his life with much abandon.

Where did Tanya fit into the larger scheme of things? He made her believe, from his life, that giving consequence to your actions is good rather than shutting out from the rest of the world. You, truly, are a citizen of the world.

Let your success as well as your vulnerability be known to the world. Be open to criticism, share your beliefs, impart your knowledge and skills, be insync with the pain. Someone, somewhere is healing with the same pain that you are suffering from and you can also, just by learning from them. Reach out to them, follow them, for the sake of your happiness.

"What are you watching?" Asha asked her, patting her on her back.

"This is my friend Tessa from high school. She's part of this Carribean cultural festival that happens every year in Canada. She dances in it, with costume et al."

"She is so hot. She is a very good dancer. " Coming from Asha, conservative and proper, it was indeed amusing.

There she was, shaking it like there was no tomorrow - swaying, twirling, teasing, breezing and owning it. Dressed in an orange costume, glistening in the sun and liming to great music with other busy-bodies. The festival consists of this big parade that happens, lots of good music, food and booze. The fete wasn't just to highlight a certain culture, but to also bring people together so that they could share their sorrows and their joys.

Tess remained to be the same "fly gyal" that she was "back in di day". Tanya knew she had also gone through her share of heartbreaks, had stagnated in her career and opted to manage a modelling agency when she was doing very well in finance.

While Neil was a guy, and guys are taught to just brush off their sorrows and be strong, women are embraced when vulnerable. We are uplifted in company of other women when sad, Tess was out there proving just that. Neither of them realized that they were contributing to Tanya' self-worth and understanding of herself in their own ways.

Similarly, when Tanya saw her own mother with the courage to move on, she felt empowered. Her mother's strong self-worth and her need to live for her kids rubbed off on her. She felt stronger and at the same time seeked to be loved, like she had been loved. Luckily, it was waiting in the wings, to happen.

She wanted to grow up to be like him, she had been sheltering her feelings, her tears and her ambitions in an effort to reinvent her life in silence, but, now, she wanted to do exactly what he was doing...

CHAPTER 22

When I miss you, I recall the tidbits about you that your family has pattered on me, smile for no reason like a dimwit, watch Selena dancing and listen to songs that help me visualize you and then miss you more.

In her mid-30s, Tanya was about as pragmatic about love as Missy is in her songs. Non-canny, shrewd, perceptive and very biased. That was her bad, though. It didn't mean that real men with compassion didn't exist. At this juncture in her life, she had learnt to live realistically and embrace herself the way she was.

His love confronted everything she had formulated to define her. For a precaurious and self-willed women like her, their encounter aroused a process of discovery that led her to the threshold of annexations. Coercing her to reevaluate her child's and her future in a sensible and assuring perspective. As Tanya and Selena embarked on their journey ahead, they realized that the one thing missing in their lives was him. They realized that where they were at present was the least that they expected they would be. A place that they had couraged themselves to reach, and it was only possible because of him.

Being in love isn't living in an illusion. It's being loved when you realize that you can't love yourself anymore than the person that loves you. It's being carried through the crummy times because you have become so unsure of your abilities that you slow-down and begin to make fallacious perceptions of yourself. Its being mended in every riven juncture in your body with his methodology and only your efforts. She realized that she would no longer feel complete without his sign *of approval. It wasn't because she wasn't independent anymore, but because he was her savior, her mendor, her affirmer...*

Purely stuff true love is made of...

There had to be a method to this madness too...smiling like a nutcase in the middle of a supermarket, while running on the treadmill or trying to finish a book right before sleeping. The more he was sorting out her life, the more delirious she was becoming.

Was this the new-age love? What was it like to date and to get to know someone at present times? In the times of dating apps and websites, you have your scope and sample in one window so that you can truly capitalize on your time and money. Men are programmed differently today, they aren't sensitized anymore to court a woman the traditional way, wait on them and let them grow into the woman's skin, so to speak. They have redefined the sentiments of quality time and bonding. Truly understandable, because the pace of life has increased like by ten-fold and to get the kind of woman you want and the life you want (happily married, big house, white picket fence, three kids, travelling), you need to be making that kind of money also. Thus, work takes priority above love. You end up forgoing alot of the initial feelings or apprehensions women have about being in your company. Tanya, back in her 20s, was warming up to this culture, there was no choice, living in one of the busiest cities in the world. The best thing about it was that men appreciated career-oriented women, women that were able to create a balance in their lives. There were the dreamers, the charmers, the practicables and the downright romantics. Sometimes though she felt really perplexed about speeding up the initial phase but was truly busy herself. Also, there wasn't like a blueprint or a script towards "the perfect courtship" leading to "the perfect romance". So there wasn't anything that ever happened gradually. You met up when you had time and then you didn't see each other for weeks, only spoke on the phone or via social media. You craved for human interaction. The standard one-liners such as: "Yo did you catch the game last night" or "Tiga is spinning at Muzik, can you and your gurls reach?" hardly sounded romantic or intriguing. The "coolios" started to seem really like the "playedouts".

Their entire understanding of a courtship was too "current" and media-driven.

Authenticity was lost, when guys could really have used this oppurtunity to woo their women with their special skills such as singing a song for them or cooking a meal for them. True definition of respecting a woman = making them a part of your life. Meaning, actually making them a part of your life, including them in your interests, making your hobbies known to them.

However, there is something so refreshing about a man that wants to take care of you, mend you and help you make your decisions. When they want to pick you up for a date, help you select your clothes or sort out your "beef" with peeps. To create an ease in your life makes them truly dependable, it really surpasses all materialistic pleasures in your equation.

Cut to present, it was Rohit, Tanya's boss' wedding anniversary, and he had bought cake for everyone on this ocassion.

"Sir, only cake, where is the full-fledged party?' Asked Humza.

"Party at my place. At 8pm. Come over for some great Biryani." He said.

"Where is the Biryani from? The usual, Stellar hotel is it?" Saira, another collegue asked.

"No. I am making it. It's usually only for my wife and her family, but tonight all of you are invited. It's a special blend of spices from both north and south."

"Amazing. I am booking a cab right away to your place, anyone want to ride with me?" Saira asked.

"Yes. We'll make it." We all said, in unison.

At about 4pm or so, Rohit was heading out. And Humza called out to him again.

"Where are you off to?" He asked.

"I am off to clean the house. "He said.

"Another gift, for her."

"Boss, tussi great ho." Humza stood up and bowed to him.

"Subeh ladayee huee hai, but I can fix any situation." We began to laugh.

"Adios. Send me your work before you guys leave." He left.

All of us sighed in the department with disbelief, and in unison. There was pin-drop silence in the room for like an entire minute.

"That is a dedicated man. Say amen, everyone." He said.

He was surely one dedicated man, according to Tanya. Dedicated because he truly wanted to make her happy. He decided to sort out the fight by helping her clean the house, that meant more to her than some gift. She must have truly felt like she could depend on him.

That truly chivalrous man, seated on a horse, racing down the crude mountains to rescue you from the goons is what true romance is made of. It wasn't only because he was strong, but because he saved her from misery.

Sadness is what happens when you are deprived of bliss. The feeling of deprivation can make you lose your focus towards peace and growth. Which is where Tanya was three years ago. Scorned from her marriage, compelled to be strong for her child and uncertain about what coarse of action to take for the future. He popped up like a muscle of vitality, robust in is convictions about her, strapping in his ardor and rugged in his protectiveness. All he asked of her was trust and to make the efforts.

Traditional in his approach, respectful enough to understand her situation and yet supafly with his sense of humor. He decided the pace at which he was pursuing her, keeping in mind that she was struggling to cope up with her father's death and managing a child in the midst of a turbulent divorce. Tanya was impressed.

Having to read, page after page, about the supposed "cruelties" imposed on her to be ex-husband by her was like physiotherapy after a fracture, more pain being inflicted on you from the outside because you are disheveled inside. It soothes you because it numbs the pain, but, your bone remains broken for days and days. It only self-heals in its own time but when given proper care. He let her heal, watching her make it from one cry to another, but never losing his focus on her.

Love in the present times also meant that couples prolonged marriage because they had goals as individuals (career, assets etc) before making that formal commitment. For him, the focus was on Tanya and Tanya only. He monitored her daily work-log, kept a close watch on her whereabouts and also began to speak to Selena, almost everyday. Getting to know Selena was the best thing about this entire "package" of a proliferant future he had envisioned with her. It was much more than she had ever felt she deserved or was capable of.

The choppy weather that surfaces when you decide to end your marriage, with speculations and advice, both pouring in equal proportions makes you want to put your child in those tough life-vests to safeguard them. Little kids aren't really more fragile but more impressionable actually, they are more prone to pick-up on all kinds of information that even you as a parent can't answer. Purely because of their age and you think they might rebel.

They are the only "constraint" while managing a smooth and successful exit from your marriage that can deviate and turn the entire thing around.

Thus the fact that he was able to intervene at the right time and initiate a bond with her so that she doesn't rebel due to the absence of a father, made Tanya more confident about facilitating the divorce process.

In today's day and age, men have, or atleast aspire to, have everything. So they don't really attach themselves onto women so quickly. Also, because of the wave of globalization and the infusion and mixing of cultures, their clusters have expanded and because of which they have become more stringent in their conditions by which they would want to commit. They are testing all kinds of locales because of it and feel like they can lessen their margin of errors.

Thus, having access to women from all around of world, in all shapes and sizes, he chose Tanya and pursued her patiently and valiantly. Everyone in her family had been applauding on his conviction and dedication. Tanya was the last one, perhaps, to be inserted into this loop because he was already speaking and getting to know her family members. Some of them, he had grown up with. This is the kind of commitment that men need to display in today's day and age. Proposing marriage to one women and making it a possibility, despite of many distractions, is the true test of chivalry and steam.

On a night out with her brother and with the littlest of her little cousins, mind you the trio had managed to annoy the living daylights out of her back in the day, were praising him in three specific words and these words only:

"Bahut accha hay....bahut accha hay...bahut accha hay".

They were wandering around, like vagabonds, on the festive streets of Hauz Khas, with persistent bouncers luring you in for a good time, bunch of delirous college kids flagging for taxis and restro-bars spewing scintillating flavors along with enrapturing music.

She was the most drunk of out the four, cuz like the protective elder sister that she was, she helped finish their drinks that they had only ordered out of a whiff. Aaah the most cherished trait of tolerance, only happens with age.!!!

It isn't the same with some good advice though, they had entered their second venue for the night and were dancing to some good-old hip-hop music, like from the 90s - when these kids could barely understand some of the slang words and Tanya was the coolest thing that ever happened to them...

"Deets (nickname for her younger brother) ...let's go upto the den area, third floor, its right above the dance floor...ask if they'll serve sheesha there."

"Okay. You guys head up there."

Smokin' away, what do four Bihari kids really talk about? Patna, saree-shopping and rickshaw rides...we were rantin away, crackin jokes...

Tanya felt so free, she hadn't been so nonchalant and uncomposed in a long time, more like, three years. Her brother noticed it.

"You feeling okay, you were the one dancing the most out there?" He asked.

"Yeah...to think I'd end up being the party-animal and you the responsible one, out of the two kids in the family. I like that I'm still the coolest in all of your eyes." She replied.

"You realize why you're so happy tonight, in your elements and yet so free." He was trying to prove a point, she could sense it.

"Yes..." She couldn't stop smiling.

"You are out here at 2.30, dancing and having a good time, while he's out there worrying until the time you get home."

"True." She said.

"Go dance if you want to....we have a good 10 minutes....we need to be home in one hour." He mentioned...

She made a dive for the dance-floor, chipper and free...

When she woke up the next morning, she had this one question in her mind...what would it be like if he was around? Would they have danced, or sat in a distant corner and talked, holding hands?

To the modern man, intimacy meant that he was being exclusive to one woman that he shared a special bond with. We must really be grateful to be living in our generation, because, we are given free will with regards to physical intimacy and informed of the consequences if we were to exercise it.

However, intimacy doesn't mean the horizontal tango, entirely. It's a mix of attraction, wit, sharpness, humor and meritorious seduction skills. You get many oppurtunities to woo your loved-one with all of these skills, the key is to make them so comfortable in your company - both physically and emotionally, that they feel like you're nothing but an extension of them. It reduces anxiety and anger because their touch calms you down, you begin to share your burdens.

What reaaly works for couples these days is to lay out your cards straight, and, then see how they unfold in the eyes of the other person. There wasn't anything hidden in Neil's eyes. In fact, his family had known Tanya's since the time neither of them were even born.

Also, for Tanya, intimacy didn't seem like a problem because she didn't only feel secure but became dependent on him because he guided her meaningfully, remained connected with her and gave imporance to her concerns...

So empowered was she under his armor, that it was her turn to make him happy. To truly live upto the expectations, never wanting to pressure her, that he had from a wife. Letting him down wasn't even an option, because he had set her free from her inhibitions. Camouflaged, she soared once again, from an incomplete urchin to an impudent butterfy...